Wallwave the Sea Prince

FLOODTIDE OF SEAWEEDS

After the murder of Waterbear, the Four Witches of Kill, with their turmoils and machinations, seek to undermine the morale of the Seagull Warriors. Queen Snakeknife and King Warchariot also sow the seeds of war between the eastern Wavewarriors and the Hillwolves of the West.

LIFE OF DREW CARSON

Sam Drew Carson was born in the North of Ireland and educated there at Wellington College and the Ulster Polytechnic. He completed his education in the USA at New Mexico Highlands University and the University of Arkansas and has traveled widely in North America, around the Atlantic and in Europe.

Drew worked as a seaman and fish-gutter in Vestmannaeyjar off the coast of Iceland. He lived and worked in the Irish and Western Isles Gaeltachts and was married in Welsh-speaking Carmarthen after which he honeymooned in Belfast. He has told his stories, composed and sung his songs, seeking storylines in Bristol and the English Westcountry. Drew has also lived and written in Nashville, Tennessee, in the wooded hills of Mid-America and from the Appalachians to the Ozarks. This was the culture that gave rise to the now worldwide Scotch-Irish country music.

In the USA, he also worked beside the bayous of the French-speaking Cajuns in the South and among the Western Spanish-speaking Navajos, Apaches and Pueblos of the Sangre de Cristo Mountains in New Mexico.

Drew has sailed far into the seas of old Gaelic and Oriental legend. After many years searching for inspiration for story and music, the author is still traveling and writing.

Wallwave the Sea Prince
ADVENTURES OF WAR QUEENS AND BATTLE HEROES

In the days before written history, clues to everyday events can be found of the existence of a chariot-based civilization in the Western Plains of Russia and Mongolia. This points to a way of life based on chariots, horses and bronze-age weapons. These clues include aerial sites, chariots, jewelry, swords and axes. Evidently the charioteers lived, died and were buried in a horse-based way of life that was more advanced in terms of chariots that had been developed up to that time.

This civilization had apparently covered much of the Asian and the Chinese as well as the Russian Western Plains. It was a pre-Celtic way of life. We do not know the name of the tribes or what language they spoke. The islands and rivers had not yet been taken over by Vikings, as happened later. How did a pre-Viking and pre-Celtic civilization develop into the later domination of the Vikings which was spread throughout eastern Europe and western Asia and Russia?

Obviously, pre-Gaelic and pre-Viking legends and myth need to be consulted. The longboats of war as well as chariots play a powerful part in these adventures. In those days the warrior queens as well as heroic Vikings played a large part.

The latter-day wars organized by Queen Bodicea of Britain who drove the Romans out of the British Isles; Queen Maeve of Connaught who led the united armies of Ireland against Ulster were similarly heroic figure. These warrior queens were field-marshals and planners of war as well as chariot warriors. Perhaps the last of this line was Saint Joan of Arc.

In WALLWAVE - THE SEA PRINCE, he builds up his armies of ships with the help of his War Queen Whitehair to defend his realm against the plots and plans for invasion laid out by the wicked War Queen Snakeknife.

BOOKS BY THE SAME AUTHOR

ZENISUB
Fun and Games in Businezz
ISBN: 978-0-9561435-2-5

GOOD FOR A LAUGH
Six Funny Playscripts for Amateurs
ISBN: 978-0-9561435-3-2

HOME WITH A GOOD COMPANION
Amateur Pantomime Scripts for a Merry Winter
ISBN: 978-0-9561435-4-9

CLASSIC EUROPEAN LYRICS
Translated from the Gaelic, the French and Spanish
ISBN: 978-0-9561435-6-3

COMMONWEALTH
An Introduction to Business Economics
ISBN: 978-0-9561435-7-0

MISSING PERSONS
Detective Felix O'Neill in a Crime Adventure
ISBN: 978-0-9561435-8-7

WEREWOLF MURDERS
Detective Felix O'Neill in a Crime Adventure
ISBN: 978-0-9561435-9-4

ORIENTAL GOVERNESS
Detective Felix O'Neill in a Crime Adventure
ISBN: 978-1-908184-00-9

LOOKING BACK
Four Nostalgic Playscripts for Amateurs
ISBN: 978-1-908184-01-6

EASTER AND THE SPRINGTIME
Five Amateur Playscripts of New Life
ISBN: 978-1-908184-02-3

WALLWAVE THE SEA WARRIOR
Adventures of War Queens and Battle Heroes
ISBN: 978-1-908184-03-0

WALLWAVE THE SEA PRINCE
Adventures of War Queens and Battle Heroes
ISBN: 978-1-908184-04-7

WALLWAVE THE SEA KING
Adventures of War Queens and Battle Heroes
ISBN: 978-1-908184-05-4

Wallwave the Sea Prince

Adventures of War Queens and Battle Heroes

BY
DREW CARSON

Order from:
https://www.createspace.com/3969927

Legals

ISBN: 978-1-908184-04-7

CONTENTS

Page

Main Characters in
The Adventures of Wallwave

SEAGULL HEROES – THE WAVEWARRIORS

Waterbear, *King of Seagulls, an oriental warrior.
Rider of the Great White Stallion (a horse with
white hair and mane)*

Seaspear, *admiral of the Hillwolves fleet,
a fieldmarshal of the sea of Wavewarrior origin*

Stormleaper, *a hero of many battles*

Whaleroarer, *a hero of fierce combats*

Icedragon, *a hero and fieldmarshal deputy*

Summersailor, *vice-king and fieldmarshal supreme,
head of Hawks battalion*

Shadowhero, *great uncle and trainer of the young*

Wallwave,* *oriental youth, son of Waterbear*
   *also known as Tsunami

Stormbolt, *younger son of Waterbear*

HILLWOLVES

Warchariot, *King of Hillwolves*

Sternrider, *supreme fieldmarshal and commander in
chief of Hillwolves and rider of the Great Bay Horse
of the West*

Winterwarrior, *deputy fieldmarshal and next in
command of the Hillwolves*

Winterfire, *the son of Winterwarrior*

Oakhill, *an assassin*

Main Characters

Cragfox, *in charge of shoreline defenses*
Flyingbat, *brother of Oakhill*
Abbott Ratrunner, *a monk who breeds rats*
The Deathhead Dwarfs, *four-eyed assassins*
The Killer Disguisers, *chamelion-like killers*

Hillwolf Queens

Queen Snakeknife, *queen of Warchariot*
Queen Spiderlair, *Warchariot's ancient mother*
Queen of Justice, *a sycophant, a false omenteller*
Queen Rainbow, *Snakeknife's mother*

Seagull Queens

Springvision, *queen of Waterbear. She has the gifts of magic and spells and discernment of spirits*
Gentleleaf, *loyal queen of Seaspear*
Whitehair, *young niece of Summersailor*
Purplelake, *sister of Summersailor*
Maplewine, *queen to Whaleroarer*
Willowflame, *queen to Icedragon*
Streamflower, *queen to Stormleaper*

Four Witches of Kill

Windweasel, *of the air*
Rivershark, *of the waters*
Meteoreyes, *of fire and hills*
Landslink, *of soil and earth*

MAIN CHARACTERS

TWO STALLIONS

Oceanhorse, *the Great White Stallion of the East*

Foresthorse, *the Great Bay Stallion of the West*

SUPERNATURALS

Truthteller, *Master of good words*

Old Washerwoman, *Diviner of omens*

Mooncrow, *a spy-bird of war*

Red Warriorwoman, *teller of fortunes*

Bullaxe, *ugly ogre with magic powers*

Firefiend, *a man of flames*

Tear, Sigh, Smile, Laugh, *the Queens from the Islands of the Everyoung*

COMBAT PERSONA

Salmon of Wisdom

Wine of Vision

*Shield of Roar, gives warning

*Bonespear, thirsts for blood

*Hardblade, a rainbow sword

   magic weapons that occasionally appear

CHAPTER ONE
A FUNERAL PLOT

Warchariot, King of the Hillwolves, and his Queen, the warriorwoman, Snakeknife, went out to seek wisdom of war.

Dressed in their full regalia of combat they rode in their battle chariots to consult with the four frail and shaky Witches of Kill, in their old lair of cold and dusty cobwebs.

There the witches made their spells to help assassins and, in return for gold, dragged down the victims to make them easy prey. Spells of delusion to make the victims hear and see strange sights of things that are not there. This was their trade, a dangerous trade, mindmadness and illusion.

The King and Queen bowed low and asked the witches, "We are plagued by the presence of Wavewarriors, fierce men in ships, who come to kill and plunder. The time has come to drive these eastern pirates back into the sea. Is it auspicious, on this dull day, to launch a just warstab to protect those who pay their tax to me?"

Then the Four Witches of Kill: Windweasel, Rivershark, Landslink and the Meteoreyes consulted themselves and put their heads together, "We have powers to help you whether the time is right or no. Let us now call upon the spirits of war and ask for their advice. We call upon the Mooncrow who is mistress of all battles and Truthteller who is master of all good words."

Then Mooncrow, the black and ugly bird of war, cawed on a rafter of the witches' lair, flew down and slowly changed its form into an old and wizened hag, her skin grown gray with age and grizzled like seal leather. Her hair was white and long-flowing, her black teeth sharp and malicious and her thin hooked nose as vicious as an eagle. Her fingers were cold as icicles hanging from the stony roof of a bat-cave.

As Mooncrow stood erect, the lightning flashed and moonbeams lit the air. Low thunder rattled and rain fell on the lair, just like the misty pall that drapes a palace when a king draws near to it on a winter's night.

The Mooncrow pointed to the clouds of darkened blood gathering over the castle. "That is the most red sunset I have ever seen, good for shepherds no doubt but surely a sign of doom, death and destruction for you and your Hillwolves."

Queen Snakeknife sneered. She was dressed as a warriorwoman decked for battle, with shield, sword, javelins, daggers around her waist. Spiked wolf-heads hung on chains upon her wrists. She was taller than anyone else in the dark room.

Snakeknife held high her head and laughed defiantly, a queenly and a haughty and a warlike laugh. Looking down upon the Mooncrow and the witches she said, "That sunset is far at sea, no doubt it bodes ill with its blood clouds for seamen and for the Seagulls and all Wavewarriors."

The four witches eagerly nodded their assent to War Queen Snakeknife.

The Mooncrow was not pleased and changed back into a bird and flew up high, once more into the rafters. Cawing, crowing and crying, "The Truthteller with his word of sword will answer you."

The Truthteller replied with a mighty clap of thunder, splitting the sky, silencing the Mooncrow and the Snakeknife. It seemed like a scream from the elephant of the universe.

There appeared before them a tall man, erect lean and wrinkled and gray-faced, the Truthteller. He held his sheaf of darts, all spoken truth. His clothing was not rich but rather plain. "I will strike you from my sheaf of trueword darts.

"My storms will rage against your fire and earth. My waters will spout against you and your fastness.

"What is this talk of war? I come to warn you that you will suffer from these plans and plots.

"Now East and West, and all men and all women, are coming together to live and trade and marry. Remember that what you send out will come back and seek you out after it has multiplied and bounced off the far wall of the universe.

"Yes, I can see the Seagulls flying out to a fertile land, out of their misty snows, from out their eastern and their northern woods from the icy wastelands where the seabears howl and claw the waves for food.

"For you, Warchariot, surely the night of the raven is at hand and you are dancing with demons of delusion.

"For now I see a horrible and bloody war where brother will kill brother and the daughter will kill her mother, nephew will kill uncle, lady will kill herself.

"For when you go to war you go to war with all your friends; not with the enemy alone but with your family. And friends will find knives for each others backs.

"War is a plague that spreads like a fierce infection. The worst disease that spreads faster than all is -

"Death."

Truthteller spoke and disappeared.

Snakeknife and Warchariot stood like warriors struck dumb who had not understood a word, nor cared.

They both had come to seek success for war and nothing else was of any interest to them.

Warchariot asked the witches, "What shall we do now about the Seagulls coming here? And how can we drive out those hungry pirates, those ravenous seasharks? How can we force them to stay where they belong, roaming and riding the fish among the icecold waves, rolling their ships along the churning green salt-smelling seaweeds with the other savage creatures of the sea, like seals, bears, whales, sharks, walrus and sharp crias?"

And Snakeknife asked, "How can we avoid a warhost invading us like a plague of hungry Seagulls? For the son of Waterbear is the Wallwave and he, the waterwall, and his storms will come to flood and pour out on our chariot warriors.

"Soon to stand up beside the waterwall will be his younger brother the Stormbolt. These things are why we need your help and wisdom.

"How are we to win advantage in this war? We do outnumber them but they have skills of combat, tricks of war-trade to help them win."

Windweasel answered, "You must kill their leader."

Meteoreyes agreed, "Your armies are made up of too many factions. Those who fight reluctantly and out of fear; those who believe the tax, that they have paid you should buy them relief from going out to war.

"In the same way the Seagulls must be split up. You must divide the Wavewarriors for they are now united in the brotherhood of sea. And all who struggle against the cold wet winds and rolling waves, the waterwalls that sweep along the green salt-smelling seaweeded sea. All these unite in a secret order, a phalanx stepping in step, with shoulder set to shoulder. But this cheap façade of order is quite breakable."

Landslink reminded him, "You, King Warchariot, you are the step-brother of the Seagull King, brave Waterbear. You must use your family knowledge and your understanding to catch him unawares and kill him then the Seagulls will surely fight over who should succeed Waterbear. Wallwave, his successor, is barely yet of age and veteran warriors will always seek to rule."

Rivershark advised Snakeknife, "Do spend and use your wealth to split the Seagull army.

"Their fieldmarshal in times of warfare is Summersailor and he is often heard to call for more support, more funds for his crack division, the Hawkarmy. Surely he can be bought for gold."

The Windweasel agreed, "Their greatest champion is the primeval seawall come alive - Wallwave, eldest son of Waterbear.

"As for the younger son, Stormbolt, leave him to us for we have magic powers and spells to tame him.

"Consider the present King, old Waterbear. If the falcon can drive the small birds to their death, if the filthy ferret can frighten the rabbits from their holes, if the mangy, miserable dogs can drive the cunning and wily fox far from his lair, then surely you and the tall Queen Snakeknife can contrive to bring great Waterbear to his downfall, to a place where he can be assassinated."

Warchariot shook his head, "He does not trust me. I am only his step-brother and long ago my mother Spiderlair cheated his father out of giving the Kingdom to his son, the Waterbear, who now rules only half of the great Kingdom that was land and sea. He would not enter any trap I set for him. Indeed I would be lucky if he would come even to my funeral and that would not help me nor help you."

Meteoreyes said, "Indeed it might help us if you were still alive and waiting for him."

Snakeknife lit up, "I see it now, a fake demise, a false funeral and a request to come and make peace and let bygones be bygones. A trap is set and Waterbear is caught."

Landslink agreed, "There is an ancient burial ceremony reserved for mighty warriors like you Warchariot. In those past days a king who died was kept lying in state in his own chariot, surrounded by his swords and spears and daggers, to be buried in a swamp and so preserved for all time in an underworld of honor. Let such a burial be yours Warchariot but let the staring eyes of the dead man be wary of who approaches him. Your faithful Queen Snakeknife will usher in the mourners of your death, including Waterbear, the

King of Seagulls, who also is your step-brother."

Rivershark eagerly agreed, "It is a beautiful thing for a warrior to be laid to rest in his battle armor, dressed and adorned with the weapons and the accoutrements of war. Resting at peace in the chariot where once he twisted and turned in the fury and the flame of hand to hand combat. How nice for the horses, of the dead warrior king, who shared his triumphs in the day of battle and faithfully led the king and his closest comrades on many a field. Those old warhorses will take their rest before the chariot as they lead the warrior to his resting place. No doubt they will return there, after their old age is past and gone, to join their friend and hero."

Tears came to the eyes of the four witches.

Then Meteoreyes spoke up, "King Warchariot, we will proclaim your death as the passing of a hero worthy of burial in a chariot of war like the ancient kings. Your step-brother, the Waterbear, will hear of this and will be likely to make peace with Snakeknife, the weeping widow, but you Warchariot will be more alive than ever you have been."

Rivershark finally explained to the Snakeknife and to the King Warchariot, "Remember, the Seagulls set their dead heroes in a ship and steer it to the West. Set it on fire to be sure that it passes to the other world, so they will understand your noble burial."

Then Warchariot went home and hid deep in his castle while his wife, Queen Snakeknife proclaimed his death to all.

CHAPTER TWO
AN INVITATION TO DANGER

There was a flowering river springing up in a fountain of fine water. Like a mist from the suns of early summertime, it danced.

In front of this wild spray of green display there stood a tall and noble king. Great Waterbear was a moderate ruler, ruling by consent with dignity and fairness to his subjects, the light of justice shining on his face. The grim glint of a protector of his people shone from his grey-blue eyes. His eyebrows bristled of black and grey and white across his forehead. His crown, his sword, his shield were silvered gold, glowing as clearly as the pale full moon stalking with pride across the palelit sky. His tunic was of linen shining like silk. He tightly gripped his spear, ready to throw it. His silver hair was curly, kingly and imperial.

On this fair island of the sea, the fortress of Waterbear gleamed in the rising sun. Brave Waterbear was the King of all the Wavewarriors and his home held many precious metals and gold and silver and gems of finest craftsmanship. Statues of gods and goddesses raised high their hands and pointed javelins and spears towards their eternal homes far in the skies.

King Waterbear and his brother Summersailor walked on the ramparts. They looked out to sea, the ocean that now separated the Wavewarriors, those Seagulls of the sun, from the hillmaster Wolves of the howling moon.

Then Summersailor pointed to the sky beyond the swirling mist, "See the smoke rise far, far over the horizon in the land of the West, of the setting sun, of speed chariots where the cruel horsemen drive the cars of death across the plains and hills. In dripping terror, knifedeadly swords and spears and axes held by mighty and fierce warriors swung owlwisely and with spirit-haughty strength. A blackbird rises and flies across the sky. See, where that smoke arises there is death and burntout bones and homes."

"Death, it is certain," agreed the swordswift Waterbear, "but perhaps that smoke is not really speaking of war. Our Seagulls would certainly have warned us of destruction or any burnings and murders and mayhem. It may be just the formal burial of a spearproud warrior. It looks to be a symbol."

As they spoke, a green and yellow bird with fine and shining feathers circled above in the sunlight. It flew slowly around flapping its wings. Then it settled with its gripping claws upon the parapet of the fastness, where it stood screeching aloud, "Come, come and see the dead."

Then the bird transformed into a woman messenger of beauty with yellow hair that flowed down upon her robes of bright green that lay around her claws.

Her sharp, black eyes stared at the Waterbear. "King Warchariot is dead and lies in state in the stone tomb below his fortress. There he sits in full accoutrements of war, a hero in his chariot evermore. Soon he will be buried and preserved in a great swamp as a memorial, just like the mighty chariotkings of old.

"Go and mourn the passing of Warchariot, your step-brother king, he whom your late father loved as fosterson and almost a kind of brother to you once. Go and comfort his widow who is alone and childless. Perhaps the Wolves, the hillmasters, will also seek you as their king of a united people.

For surely this is the purpose of your kingship that both our peoples may again unite.

"Enter your longboat and swiftly sail away to talk of peace. The cautious Wolves would never permit a fleet to enter in upon them for fear they might be hacked with swords and broken, defeated and enslaved by their old foes. But if you come alone, clearly in peace, perhaps they will unite our warring peoples. Let your longboat spring up through foaming waves cutting like shark through seaweed, swift and knifedeadly.

"Of course, you may go armed for self-defense. You and a small troop in your battleboat, flashing with bows and arrows and broad axes, threatening a rain of javelin thrusts, the hail of sun spears, flying daggers, sticks of torment - fearing no man on earth to block your way."

The bird of message laughed and spread her claws and shook her arms like wings and flew away.

Then Springvision, wife of brave Waterbear, came out into the sunlight from the shadows. Springvision was long and pale and soft as silk. Her lips were like purple berries wet in snow. Like a slim sapling of a beautytree. Her fragile robes like leaves upon the branches.

"I saw and heard it all," said Springvision, "The wind is cold. Let us go down below and talk about this message from a bird. Let us consider what is behind this omen."

In the great sunroom of the palace, War Queen Springvision spoke to brave Waterbear and to his brother the Summersailor who was second in the kingdom. "They will never let you approach with a large force sufficient for your protection. They have said so, because they fear you. Why should they so fear if they would seriously consider you for their king? What nonsense! It is a snap-trap. Do not go. If you are killed, all mayhem will break loose. Your son Wallwave will return and rule, for he will need to bring peace to the land and well may perish in the strife and turmoil."

"Calm down my dear wife," replied the Waterbear, "Our son Wallwave is fully grown and needs no training, more than the edge of real life combat-sword experience. For courage is the best training for a warrior and even our younger son Stormbolt has courage aye and skills too, far beyond his years. Besides, my duty to honor my step-brother's rank brings honor to my own rank as a king. Although at enmity with him while still alive, death is the door that opens up new visions. Also, my dear wife, there is no one who is strong enough to frame a plot against me, now that the chariot king is dead and gone.

My brother's warriors will be in a state of chaos and fighting each other for the throne. Who knows, perhaps I can become kingmaker if not the king and broker the cause of someone friendly to us. And do not fear that I seek a second wife, for I have no such need. You have been all that I have ever loved, my wife, Queen Springvision."

"I know, I worry for your life not your devotion. I do not trust your step-mother or step-brother for your step-mother, the witch Spiderlair, was so crowngreedy that she married the old king just to steal his crown. And tell me, what were brothers ever good for but mutual murder in a bond of jealousy? Crossbreeding leads to peace they say, but falsely. Crossbreeding leads to envy and resentment, for intermarriage is a two-edged sword, one blade for law, the other edge for war. Is it to be for peace or enmity within the gates? Who knows? So take no risks."

"My father King Snowcurl and his usurping Queen, who stole the crown, are dead. Now dead also is his adopted son Warchariot, so let those old usurpers lie in peace."

Springvision shook her head sadly and said, "Warchariot's deadly wife, Snakeknife, is still alive and well."

But Waterbear replied, "So let there be a case for just forgetting."

Then Springvision threw herself upon the floor, "Please, please, my husband do not leave me here as you mourn a mere usurper and a coward. Remember how Warchariot stole his kingdom from the old king of the world, Snowcurl your father, when you should have been the true inheritor?"

"That was the work of Spiderlair, my witch-stepmother. It was she who was the schemer, the usurpress and not Warchariot."

Queen Springvision addressed the viceking, Summersailor, "And you too, Summersailor, you were also cheated by your step-mother's cunning and deceitful plot. Remember that you are the second warrior brother who was cold-bloodedly disinherited when the old queen stole the kingdom for her son. Your father was the king of hills and isles, rivers and waterfalls and faraway shores. Even as the younger brother, you might well have come to rule one half of all the kingdom but now you are the vi-king of brave Waterbear thanks to the Spiderlair's machinations and deception."

"My father Snowcurl is the one to blame for marrying a widow with a son.

"Yes, I will marry you she told my father when she and he were both mature in age. Why could my father not have been content to live a single life when my dear mother, Silvercheek, the Queen of the World, had passed away? What spells, what evil potion, what illusions caused him to lust for ancient bones and wrinkles, gray hairs, withered claws and toothless kisses?"

Then the Summersailor drew his fiercepoint sword and threw it hard into the palace wall. "What lies and cunning witchery stole one half of all the kingdom?"

Waterbear then spoke, "And yet no blood was spilled. Our father was not wise but only good and strong and trusting, drinking of witches brews that caused delusion. He saw his new wife as a girl of beauty."

Springvision laughed in mockery and derision, "Beware that witchery still lingers on in such a greedy and deceptive clan of kill."

Then Springvision wept and then entreated more, "A woman, past her best, ancient and haggard comes to the king of many lands and seas. I will marry you if you give my son the title, the title only, of king for one brief year. Old Spiderlair is a lean and crafty usurper who comes to steal away the throne. The king marries the witch and gives her son the title, imagining that he has won a girl of beauty, delusioned as he is by smells and brews of flowers and herbs and greeneries and haziness and words of magic muttered in the mists of devilry and demons seizing power. Oh, what a fool."

"Yet, aren't we all at times," said Summersailor, "If only we could see what dangers lie ahead, we could all choose the better and the clearer ways of life.   But we cannot always see reality.

"So when the people saw that Snowcurl, my old father, had married a witch and given her greedy son the title of a king, even for one year, they saw Snowcurl deluded by witches' spells and the people lapsed into a state of uneasy enmity among themselves.

"Within the year Warchariot found it no trouble to divide us and to conquer while, brave Waterbear and I as the sons of Snowcurl, were waiting with respect for him to die and leave the kingdom of the world to one of us. Then the witch's son, Warchariot, no relative by blood of any of us and his thieves raided our armories. They stole our weapons, chariots and horses, leaving us only ships and tools of war and all the smaller hand weapons. Yet they stole the one and most important thing that we as princes had ever owned, our people's simple trust."

"That," agreed Springvision, "has split the kingdom now and forever. Since we sailed away to hold the seas and isles and cold and remote places, the warriors of King Snowcurl have been divided into two peoples. Some are birds and fishes on one side and on the other some are fleet land creatures fleeing the seas and the waterwalls.

Humanity is split in two. Dark forces on one side are the fields and hill volcanoes, fire and earth. On the other side the powers of air and sea.

"The dark forces have the witches that dwell in caves of bats. We have the master of all good words to help us, although rarely does he bestir himself to save a life. We are almost alone in this great world of warfare and none of us should ever dare to trust the liars and thieves who stole our throne by stealth. You well may go, my husband, with good reasons but you will not return I fear, as easily.

"Stay here I beg you, Waterbear, and soon we will have built up our weaponries of battle. When our two sons, Wallwave and Stormbolt, are fully trained and our men are well equipped, let our longboats spring up through foaming seas, cutting like sharks through the seaweed, swift and knifedeadly. We will flash with bows and arrows and broad axes. We will threaten a rain of javelin thrusts, the trail of sunspears, flying daggers, sticks of torment. We will fear no man on earth to block our way."

And Summersailor agreed, "Yes, stay with us. There is no need to go and mourn with Snakeknife."

But Waterbear replied to his wife and brother, "I am restrained by my duties as a king to bring prestige and peace to all my people. If I do not go as a single warrior, if I do not go at once in deepest mourning, I will be called cowardly or devious."

"If you do go and are killed, you will be a fool just like your father. No good can come of this."

"That is not so, Springvision. Perhaps I can restore the kingdom of the world to unity. Moon against sun, East against West, land against seas, bird and fish against the great earth creatures is a strange and unnatural configuration. Perhaps I can unite them now that the usurper Warchariot is dead . . ."

"So witches tell and you believe their lies."

Then seeing that her warnings and words were of no avail, Springvision went away and looked out over the dark sea and wept.

Waterbear turned to his younger brother Summersailor, "My brother, I am mid-aged and soon must die in any case. If I do not return I leave my kingdom to my eldest son, Wallwave. He is to reign and one day marry Whitehair, your fair niece. A fit match for my son, we must agree. In that way you will be the uncle of a king and a warrior niece who is a queen."

And the Summersailor agreed with Waterbear, "Just so, my elder brother. This is agreed. I will look forward to their reign one day."

Then Springvision came back and composed herself. She sat and shook her head, "Here we all sit," she wept, "and make our future plans and hopes. So who will marry whom? Who will inherit the kingdom? Maybe we will unite the world once more under our throne. Yet, if you go and risk your life among the treacherous followers of the usurper, Spiderlair, there will be no future for us or our children. We cannot see the future from this forest. So let us just be wise and hope and pray.

"Stay home brave Waterbear and build our kingdom, not trusting any of the powers of greed nor those who bring destruction on the earth. Then, let us think of marriage and success and joy, for all our children and our children's children, free from the risks of war that you leave open."

Summersailor was pleased with all these wise words, "I look for success from all the spirits of kindness that rule and reign throughout our universe. Though they are slow to help us in this life, yet do I swear by them and not another.

"Yes, I will pray that you and your young sons and I and all the rest of us will be safe and prosperous. I will be vigilant and not let down my sword or spear or axe.

"All my loyalty has ever been to you, my elder brother, as you well know. I will try to keep the promises I make.

"On this great day I swear my allegiance to you and yours, great Waterbear. My blood is yours to spill and yet we must be careful. Our mighty ships and our great Hawkarmy, the crack division, pride of all our troops, are scattered and need food and weaponry."

And Waterbear replied, "Take the command of the whole crack division, known as the Hawkarmy. While I am gone away upon this mission, I appoint you to be their fieldmarshal for life if I should not return to take my place. But then all is not yet lost, for I will return I do believe and take back the command and so demote you."

Summersailor smiled, "May it be so," he said and they shook hands.

The sun slunk silverly and silently behind a cloud.

CHAPTER THREE
MURDER OF A KING

Springvision saw that her warnings and wisdoms were of no avail so she went away and sent for her messengers. "Take wing I say and bring to me my son Wallwave who now dwells far, far away, swimming with sharks in the great eastern sea. Beneath the waves he learns and practices the crafts of duel with sharptoothed lionfish. The supernatural one who watches over him is the Truthteller, his godfather and teacher.

"Tell him that his father Waterbear grows old and is no longer owlwise and spirithaughty and needs the Wallwave's help in war and wisdom."

Then the messenger took the form of a great seagull, flapped her white wings and flew into the East.

Springvision looked far into the sea for wisdom.

Brave Waterbear put on his battle armor, his sword and shield and spear and axe and dagger and all his other accoutrements of combat.

Then he called Springvision to his side and kissed her, saying, "Farewell, but just for now. For I am confident that I will return and you will see me standing in my ship, sailing into this harbor in the mists. I will come home once more with duty done."

And Springvision put her head upon his shoulder and warned him to beware of his step-family.

The king called to his side his close attendants and set sail in his longboat for the burial ceremony. As the stately rowers gently steered the boat out of the harbor, there suddenly appeared upon the shore the figure of an old washerwoman. She was dressed in red robes, her face shriveled and ugly, wailing and weeping as she washed her clothes and pounded them upon the redstained rocks. The rowers paused and all looked at the woman as she wrung red blood from every sheet and garment, red flowing away from her like a river of slaughter.

"What do you see, old woman?" asked the Waterbear, "Whose garments do you wash?" he asked the crone.

"I wash your clothes. I wash your vest of wool. See the white wool as cool as mountain snow; see how it flows away from me in blood. I rinse white shirts in water clear as crystal and it flows away from me as a river of thick and bubbling living blood, hot to the touch."

"What of my son, you seer?" asked Waterbear.

"Your son, Wallwave, rests deep in the eastern seas watched over by his godfather, Truthteller, ruler of seas and winds. Wallwave will win many battles above all your foes. It is said that the father sows and the son reaps," the withered, wrinkled frail old hag replied, "Turn back; it is not too late to flee your fate."

Then the vision of the prophetess grew vague and hazy and disappeared into the misty air.

As Waterbear watched her go, he told his men, "Vague prophecies mean little. What if I sow wild seeds of victory in the blood of others? She sees the victories for my son to reap.

"Yet, all vile witches are on the side of the Wolves. It has been known for a long time that witches are plotting devious and scheming plans to make sure that the Seagulls are driven out, while the Wolves take up the lordship of all lands. Why would they want to warn us of defeat or try to help us in anyway at all? If these grim witches warn us not to travel then some great triumph for us must lie ahead. Let us go forward always in peace, I say."

Yet, at this time, the Waterbear did not hear the laughter in the air of sniggering witches. Brave Waterbear forged ahead in his longboat, proudly as a hero going to pay his homage to another hero who had died in peace.

The Waterbear stood upright in the prow, his eyes looking ahead and his arms folded, a worthy king, royal, keeneyed and brave, a fiery, sunlike visage, red of hair on head and face. His beard was forked and pointed, the thick red hair flecked with yellow where it was cut sharply across the nape.

Around his shoulders there draped a cloak of purple silk, pinned down by a bright broach of wrought gold shaped like seagulls. Next to his skin he wore a shirt of satin and on his left arm there was clipped a shield of purple brown with yellow gold agleaming around the rim.

In his left hand he held a spear and javelins, smooth and well formed for throwing. They gleamed threateningly with purple sharpness. His right hand rested on the golden hilt of a silver sword, fine carved with fish and birds. There was no warrior upon the earth more ready or stronger with lightning movements to leap upon the enemy and strike.

In his long reign as king of all the Seagulls, his kingdom, although driven out to islands and remote shores, was blessed with many fountains, streams, vines and farms that all flourished with foods and fish and fruits and milk and honey.

His kingdom stretched from West to East far into the land of the rising sun, subduing waterfalls and fire volcanoes, flaming out in spite. So he was feared and obeyed by many nations who paid him their obedience and their homage.

Now far towards the red setting dusk he sailed, past many islands, many shores and rocks. Round about his head the seagulls screamed and the crias sang aloud as falcons swooped like a flying crown of champions around his head.

Soon he arrived at the castle of Warchariot. It was surrounded by cruel crocodiles in the moat but soon the drawbridge was lowered to receive him. Thus Waterbear and his troop arrived to mourn, with dignity and respect, the death of Warchariot.

The castle of Warchariot was also in mourning, with windows darkened by long dismal curtains and the faces of the servants were drawn and dark, for Snakeknife, the Queen of Warchariot had announced his death. Yet the mourners and all the nobles and the heroes of the Hillwolf kingdom were intent on drinking and making merry, laughing and eating with dancers, dwarfs, jugglers and joyful singing. This was a wake that well could have been continued, after the death of Waterbear had been achieved. Indeed, it was a feast designed to last for many days after the funeral. But no one, other than Queen Snakeknife, knew that King Warchariot lived and laid in wait.

Then servants and attendants were sent to Waterbear and his small group, bringing them music, dancers, strong sweet-scented drinks and savories.

The small group all partook of these enchantments except Waterbear. He stood aloof and waited until the darkcowled Snakeknife approached and bid him welcome to the funeral. She was falsely weeping and sorrowing with her two waiting ladies, one on each arm.

Waterbear murmured his respects, "Condolences my lady, I am most sorry."

"Thank you. My husband asked that you should come to mourn and to memorialize his funeral so that our two peoples may be at peace."

Dismissing her attendants, she spoke softly, "Come, I am going to his funeral chariot down these stone steps, to the lying-in-state basement from which he will be borne away for burial in a deep swamp, just like the kings of old."

Then Waterbear, like a true king, upright and dignified, with weapons and his shield still proud upon him, followed the grieving widow dressed in her flowing, darkest weeds and veils, down the steep steps into the pit of peril.

Down in the stone room of lying in state Warchariot sat upright in his chariot in full regalia, like kings of old. His eyes stared straight ahead. Around the walls, beside the spears and shields for a long battle, were bits and bridles and trappings of two horses and urns of eastern craft for drinking wine.

King Warchariot's face was painted white and black. He wore all his accoutrements of combat: his silver shoulder pieces and his helmet; his boots and armlets bright with burnished mail; his belts and buckles for his knives and dirks; his silver helmet with a neckshield of bronze. Set firm along his round brass shield of war, at his left side, were three lances and a sword. In his right hand was a large and shining dagger.

Only three candles burned in the burial chamber. A roar of revelry and making merry and singing could be heard coming from above. The dark-veiled widow knelt beside the body and bowed for prayer to the gods of war.

Waterbear also knelt down beside the false widow and bowed his head as a token of respect.

Suddenly Warchariot raised his dagger and struck deep into the back of the bowed down Waterbear. The blade sank through the cloak and purple tunic till the knifetip showed at the heart of Waterbear who fell in agony and gasped and died.

War Queen Snakeknife tore the dark veils from her face and from her body and threw them to the floor; for underneath she wore a bright silken dress. Screaming with joy, she danced up the tomb steps and joined the dancers and the drinking.

Then Warchariot appeared at the top of the tomb steps holding across his arms the bleeding body of Waterbear. The merriment fell silent as horror struck the mourners and the servants as they realized that they had been an unwitting party to such a murder. They stared with fear until the Waterbear was taken by his servants to his ship. After the dead Waterbear had gone, the mourners took again to laughing and singing and dancing.

Shocked and mind-blown, like the walking dead, the small stunned troop of Wavewarriors sailed back and bore the body of their leader Waterbear home to the palace of the Seagull Warriors.

So the grieving Springvision placed the body of her dead husband Waterbear in a longboat filled with sword and axe and javelins. She set up Waterbear in his best tunic and in his armor for head and chest and limbs, decked in his full accoutrements of war.

Then the boat and sails and body were set on fire as the rudder was fixed to sail due west as the Wavewarriors sent it sailing to the Isles of Youth.

Unseen by the others, Springvision stole out to a great crag overlooking the burning ship and leapt into it to be with her loved husband on his last journey. And so she perished with him.

CHAPTER FOUR
TESTS OF COURAGE, SKILL AND TRUTH

Now in those days it was the custom of the warlords to hone and harden up their sons, to sharpen them by putting them out to fosterage among the poor who fight among themselves for every scrap of food. And in this way the warlord's sons grew up alert in mind as well as quick in reflex and suspicion of all attackers coming from any direction.

The warlord's son also received good food, given to the foster parents by the warlord.

The foster son also was given good training in all the many arts of battlecraft and the skilled use of many weapons of war by a related older warrior, a veteran or perhaps a grandfather or a great uncle.

The foster parents and their children benefited not only by receiving foods and gifts from the warlord but they also gained a friend and a protector in their foster son. So the foster family moved from poor to middle as the young warrior finished his long training.

At this time Stormbolt, who was the younger warrior son of Waterbear and Springvision, lived far away in northern caves and waves with his foster family. His trainer in all the arts of battlecraft was his greatuncle Shadowhero.

Stormbolt was almost twenty years of age and close to mastering all the feats and tricks, the leaps and jumps and twists and thrusts and parries, of hand-to-hand hard combat. Yet, when the message of the death of Waterbear was sent by a great white albatross to

Shadowhero, he wept but could not bring himself to tell the bad news to his grandnephew, young Stormbolt.

So Shadowhero, that gnarled, old and kindly warrior, the greatuncle of Stormbolt and Wallwave, told himself that Stormbolt had seen little of his true father. In this way, Stormbolt had loved more and looked to his foster family as his own and so he needed just a few more weeks of training to hold his own as a hero on the battlefield.

Shadowhero did not tell the young Stormbolt about the murder of brave Waterbear. For Shadowhero was old in mind and body and merely told young Stormbolt, "Bear with me, for I have received a message that concerns you. It was sad news but you must not know of it until you have completed all your training in a few weeks or months. So train yourself and I will guide your skills. You will need courage when I inform you of the truth, I know."

"Why do you weep and what was that white bird?" The boy asked.

Yet the grand old veteran could not tell Stormbolt of his father's death in case the boy might perish in an attempt to avenge his father's murder by Warchariot. He hoped another warrior or the hand of fate might soon avenge the murder of Waterbear.

Shadowhero withheld the message and so failed to meet the standard of a champion in warfare, the tests of courage, skill and truth.

***

The red sun rose above the eastern sea as an albatross informed the elder son, the Wallwave, of the death of Waterbear in cunning treachery.

Then far beneath the waves there was a rumbling as a wallwave rose in a mighty wave that shattered all before it towards the west and drowning ten thousand fishermen in boats.

Watched over by his godfather the Truthteller and riding this mighty tidal wave, Wallwave in his longboat now sailed upon the crest to avenge the assassination of his father.

But now his eyes were set upon fierce combats, for first he had to claim his rightful place as king and leader of all the Seagulls. What could one single warrior do against the might of murderers unless he had the support of all his army? Warchariot's killers were always ready to strike in treachery or treason and with claws of witches lurking in the gray background.

Yet Wallwave's sword and shield and gleaming javelins shone in the light of the morning dawn like stars of heaven gathering their spears together.

Wallwave's yellow skin glowed like his shield of bronze; his dark brown eyes like dagger points set deeply in the keen gashes of his face, his was nose like a great eagle's searching its prey.

He was an oriental prince of air and water. Swifter and more spirithaughty and proud, fiercer and more terrifying and owlwise than many an older and more experienced warrior was the searush of Wallwave's mindfury as his longboat sped along on the wavewall's back.

***

Meanwhile, at the palace of the Seagulls, sad Summersailor mourned the death not only of Waterbear and Springvision but also the death of peace and order, law and succession among the Seagulls as they strove and argued among themselves as to who would succeed Waterbear. For many would not accept the young Wallwave and some argued to await the coming of age of Stormbolt and some argued for the Summersailor.

Many fine champions came to the Seagull Castle in hopes of setting themselves above the rest or at least finding a high and preferred place with the new warlord, whoever he might be.

In the vast champion's palace there were rooms for a hundred warriors and their lovely queens. In the great hall the throne was red but empty. Each fine apartment was paneled in red yew; red for the blood that bought the hall for freedom. Along the walls were javelins, shields and swords twinkling like stars of gold. The silver glimmered on the necks and coils of copper javelins, on the embosses and the rims of mighty shields, on the chalices and goblets and the drinking horns.

Servants and attendants, cooks and wine bearers, tables and chairs and couches filled the palace. Behind the empty throne stood heads and trophies, weapons and jewels and finest pins and broaches, of enemies long past and dead forever.

Beside the throne, for privacy in the making of royal commands, stood mighty screens of copper. These screens were all decked with gold and silver birds whose eyes were jewels, picked out and polished and long traveled from all over the world. These were the whispering screens of kingly secrets.

Behind the empty throne a huge oak door led to the barred and bolted and forbidden treasury of weapons. Here was a store of wealth in priceless gems and gold and silver ornaments gleaming on the accoutrements of combat.

***

A gray mist dropped like a pall upon the palace like a vague vestment covering a coffin. Underneath the pall a festering swamp rose up out of the earth with sharp foul smells.

Out of the swamp there strode an ugly oaf, a huge man, fat of mouth, heavy of shoulder, panting and puffing like a buffalo. His eyes were baggy and his face was bristling with sharp gray stubble and thick bushy eyebrows. His face was well wrinkled with thick hanging skin and on his head, dark short-cropped patchy hair. His teeth were blunt, black, misshapen and uneven.

As the Wavewarriors gathered in the palace, the oaf's footsteps made the earth to quake and quiver. The trophies shook on the wall, trembling and jingling. The monster clomped and lumbered slowly and clumsily in his green leathery shoes as he entered the hall before the great assembly. He slouched forward, eight feet tall with a thick neck and head. His eyes bulged out and his flat nose was snorting like a great bull, dressed up in human guise. His arms and legs were caked with soil. He carried across his arms a huge and gleaming axe as long as any warrior and four feet in breadth. Its blade was curved and sharp, keen as a razor.

The smell that hung around his body was like that of weeds from an old heap of dung or from flowers and bushes that hung around his head or from his coat of tree's bark, leaves and branches. On his sleeve were the yellow and green cuffs of an oaf.

"I am Bullaxe," he roared. "I have come to this assembly of champions who would be king to test if any one man can be found to keep his word. One man of skill and courage is all I ask. Yes, I have searched the world and never could I find one man of courage with skill and honor.

"All warriors have failed me. I ask because you have need of such good men to be your generals and to be your new king now that the brave Waterbear has been so brutally murdered. You need a man of guts and skill and truth, for who can live with bunglers, liars and assassins?"

"You have spoken well but who is fit to judge these virtues of a king?" asked the Summersailor, "Who are you, Bullaxe, to judge?"

The ogre raised his hand, "Silence," he roared. "You all will judge. I bring only a test. It is a test of fairness, courage and skill. I say, accept my simple challenge, Tit for Tat, Turn and Turnabout and Blow for Blow. That's a fair deal. That is an honest bargain. Let's have it so, a Blow for Blow fair deal. O let's have fun and all can be agreed on This for That. So you do yours and then I will do mine. O we'll have such happy fun."

The company relaxed and many asked "What are these children's games that you propose?"

"O yes, it's fun," the ogre roared, "It's just that I cut off your head tonight, then you come back tomorrow night and cut off mine. You see it's just a test of courage, skill and honor. Let's see if you have the skill to take my head, the courage to face up to me, the honor to come back here tomorrow as agreed so that you in turn can chop off my poor head."

"This is all nonsense, for how can any man keep his appointment when he is dead?" cried Summersailor. "Go back to your black hole. You are a filthy fool."

The ogre Bullaxe paused for breath and thought. "Stop. Ha, Ha, I do see what you mean. So you go first. Whichever way, it is all right with me. Let any warrior chop off my head tonight. See? Then I will come and chop off his tomorrow. Yes, Tit for Tat is anyway you want it. And Head for Head, my head your head, is fair. So what's the difference in who goes first? Let any man who would be king go first. Ha, Ha, we'll have such fun and games tonight."

Fireball, an obscure warrior and little known, who was ambitious and impetuous, spoke up to stake his claim upon the championship. "Then I go first. I will chop off your head right now and you can chop off my head tomorrow."

So Bullaxe cleared a circle before the fire and moved a log into the centre of it, handed his mighty axe over to Fireball and lay face down with his neck upon the log and submissively and mildly closed his eyes. Fireball took hold of the massive axe with difficulty and raised it high above the head of Bullaxe.

The company stood quite still and gasped in horror as Fireball brought down the axe with all his might upon the ogre's neck but did not sever it, achieving only a deep gash upon the side where blood poured out and spurted in a stream.

Some of the ladies were shocked at the sight of the blood. They turned themselves into seagulls and flew up into the rafters, screeching in terror, as Bullaxe rose up and shook his fists at them.

"Small sympathy I get when I am mutilated," he railed at them.

Then he turned to Fireball and seized back his axe from the unconqueror, "Bungler and weakling, you have broken the bargain. You have not cut off my head. Now play the game. Let us be fair and not torment each other."

Bullaxe seized Fireball by the throat and threw him over the log and cut off his head. "Your wound was merely puerile. Cut off my head next time properly, decently and cleanly."

As the blood poured out from the neck of Bullaxe, he cried in a loud voice, "Here is my axe. Let any man take it into his hand. Will any man be man enough to behead me right now and I will behead him tomorrow night? Accept this simple challenge, Tit for Tat, Turn and Turnabout, Head for Head, an honest bargain."

So the Wavewarriors whispered among themselves, "The ogre is insane and who knows what magic he has in mind for us. Who knows who sent him here or for what strange reason? Let us get rid of him and all his hatreds."

Then a Seagull shot an arrowbolt at Bullaxe from a crossbow. Bullaxe seized the bolt like a child swatting a mosquito in the air and threw it back to the bowman, splitting his head, killing the loosebolt bowman instantly. After that, no one dared to shoot a missile at Bullaxe.

So the ogre ranted, "Quick, do let me die now, please cut off my head and let me cut off yours tomorrow night."

"I say he must be mad," cried out Summersailor, "a renegade of the moon

willing to let anyone cut off his head."
Summersailor came to the conclusion
that Bullaxe really was prepared to die.

His henchmen whispered quietly
to Summersailor, "You can take him. If
you can get his head he cannot rise to
strike again for once he's dead, he's
dead. This will be glory for you."

So Summersailor cried out to the
ogre. "Calm Bullaxe and forgive us now
for allowing only Fireball to play this
game with you. He was a quick and
courageous warrior but as for skill and
strength, not quite the best. Forgive us
for not sending out our champion. I am
the first of all Wavewarriors. Next to
the young now faroff Wallwave, who is
not here, I am the supreme one. I will
cut off your head tonight and you may
cut off mine tomorrow night if that is
quite acceptable to you. If you are not
too wounded to endure it."

Then Bullaxe laughed loudly. "Me
get wounded? What a joke! I like to

play my game of Head for Head. It is such fun and fair and elegant."

Whitehair, niece of Summersailor, stood slender and delicate, a thoughtful lady, pure as a swan and wise as a nightowl. She spoke quietly to her uncle, "Do not do this; this is an evil bargain and steeped in witchcraft. You would do better to ignore his cruel raving. I beg you, Uncle, do not play this game. The Tit for Tat of Bullaxe is not fair."

Summersailor whispered to his niece, "There is no danger. Once he's dead, he's dead."

Whitehair replied, "The wicked never die, they live forever . . . in filthy forests, the home of all ugly spirits. Take care, my uncle."

But Summersailor paid no heed.

Then Bullaxe cleared a circle before the fire and moved a log into the center of it, handed his mighty axe over to Summersailor and lay facedown with his neck upon the log, submissively and smiling, closing his eyes. Summersailor took hold of the massive axe with ease and raised it high above the neck of Bullaxe.

Whitehair drew back and turned her head in horror as her uncle, Summersailor, with all his might, brought down the axe upon the neck of Bullaxe and severed the head sharply from its body. Some of the ladies shrieked and changed their form into the guise of seagulls, flying and fluttering into the rafters high above.

The head of Bullaxe rolled over on the floor and screamed in pain as blood poured out from eyes, ears, nose and mouth and from its severed neck.

In agony, it swore revenge on the Summersailor. "Tomorrow I will repay you for this torment," spat out the head and then began to laugh and chortled, "Ha, Ha, only joking friends. What fun and fairness that will be for me."

Bullaxe stood up and taking back his axe from Summersailor and lifting up his head from off the floor, and clutching his head, still bleeding, to his chest he straightened up and the head spoke to Summersailor, "You have great courage for agreeing to my bargain. You have skill for chopping off my head so cleanly. But do you have the honor and the truth to come back here tomorrow night so that I can chop off your head as we have agreed? Tit for Tat and Head for Head. Our bargain."

Then Summersailor grew faint and dizzy with fear and fell back as the ogre's head spoke out, moaning and bleeding from underneath his arm.

With axe in one hand and his head in the other, with blood still streaming down his chest and falling upon the floor, the ogre turned away and muttered casually, "Bit of a breeze is brewing up from the seadeep, perhaps it's a wallwave."

The head laughed. "Ha, Ha, Ha." The warriors standing by were silent and stood stunned beyond all words with fear and disbelief.

Then Whitehair fainted into the arms of the warrior ladies who attended to her.

And the severed head of the ogre sneered and winked at the seagulls hiding high in the metamorphoses brought upon them by their terror.

The head sneered, "You will be glorious in days of war to come."

But as he lumbered out of the silvery palace, clutching his head and axe, the head screamed, "Tomorrow night, my turn to behead you, in honesty and integrity and justice. You who would be the commander of the Wavewarriors. Be here and ready great Summersailor, the brother of King Waterbear. See you keep your word."

Then, stinking of clotted blood, the severed head under his arm called out defiance to the Wavewarriors, as the ogre tramped back to his swilly swamp.

CHAPTER FIVE
THE WALLWAVE COMES

Then the gathered Wavewarriors in the Seagull Palace went to their rooms to sleep. As the night fell, a great storm from the sea began to brew. Waves of salt seawater leapt up high. The wind growled out. A low baritone of thunder grumbled innocently in the far isolated distance. It was just a polite and genteel cough, an incidental cough and a mere clearing of the deep waters throat.

But yet how treacherous, lying and deceitful can a seaweed tempest be? For very soon, small colored creatures fled. Rabbits and foxes, dogs and mice and cats, scurried away from the low-lying fields, along the shore, to creep into the higher ground of trees and caves and bushes in the hills. There to burrow and hide quietly from the wallwave which now began to stir and roar and flood jungles of sea and land. And Summersailor joined them to hide from Bullaxe and his bargain.

A sharp shout from the fierce sea storm's tongue spread out across the forest hills and slopes in a cold, cold blast as the giant of the deep roared out his grief and imminent revenge.

The next evening, as stormwaters lapped around the palace floors, all the warriors gathered in the palace to see if the Bullaxe would reappear.

In the fort, Whitehair awaited the return of the Wallwave.

"Look," cried the watchman from the parapet, "The ogre is returning, clomp upon clomp; he walks like one possessed by anticipation; he stomps here eagerly in search of heads.

"See, he is whole. His head back on his shoulders and his head and neck is unmarked on his body and just as though it never had been severed.

"As large as life and twice as natural, he lumbers inexorably towards our fortress."

Then the watchman turned into a frightened seagull and flew into the rafters, there to screech. Some warriors closed and barred the great front door.

So Bullaxe appeared once more, kicked down the door and entered. His breath was putrid and his look was mean, nasty, destructive and ugly. He was seeking and searching like a big bully looking for a child to murder.

His arms were thick and muscular and powerful with wiry sinews ready to squeeze out life from any creature. A hard and cruel yokel whose butt stuck out like a tree trunk well behind him. He was a swaggering, arrogant and audacious, filthy oaf.

Bullaxe peered around at the warriors and sneered and roared aloud,

"Step forward Summersailor, it's my turn now. How I am going to enjoy this fun of beheading. Its a test of fairness, courage and skill. I say, accept my simple challenge – Tit for Tat.

"Where are you Summersailor? Only last night you chopped my head off, now I will enjoy chopping your head off. It is a fair bargain. Oh let's play games Summersailor. Where are you?"

And the ogre held his axe out at the ready, but Summersailor was hiding away in the high hills.

Then War Queen Whitehair, the niece of the Summersailor, spoke out. She was slender and delicate, a thoughtful lady, pure as a swan and wise as a nightowl, "My uncle is not here nor should he be. You speak of fairness but magic is not fair and you are practicing some kind of magic."

Bullaxe answered, "I am here to set a test of championship. To test and to uphold guts, skill and truth and to expose the cowards, bunglers and liars. No one will ever win who fears to die. Your uncle is a liar and a coward. The people of the Wavewarriors have excelled all other people in power and in rank: in weaponry and all the arts of battle: in truth and generosity and dignity.

"People all fear you. Can I not find a warrior, even one among you who will keep his word? Where is your family honor and integrity?"

Then Whitehair answered, slender and delicate, pure as a swan and wise as a nightowl, pointing her long, slim finger at Bullaxe, "He stands behind you listening to your rant."

The ogre turned and crouched, twitching his axe. "What flotsam has the storm washed up?" he roared and laughed with joy to see the slim Wallwave.

There in the open doorway of the palace the ogre saw Wallwave, armed for battle, his skin a yellow-glowing in the sun. The water and the seaweed dripping from him glittered and glowed among his golden weapons. Although raw and young, he was ready for war. Ready for any battle combat was this eastern warrior. On his sleeve there shone the red cuffs of a champion. Across his chest there hung a waterhorn. Around Wallwave's head hero-light shone and small birds flew in the halo. Aromas, flowers and foliage and seaweed hung in the air; the smells of afterstorm were strong around the Wallwave. Even the ogre held his breath to see him and stepped back, but not in fear, only in respect and awe.

"What do you want of me?" asked the Wallwave.

And Bullaxe answered with a thick stabbing finger, "Your father's brother has not kept his bargain to let me take his head, after he had beheaded me last night. Therefore your clan and all your people are today dishonored by his craven fear of death. So go your way and join the ranks of cowards to be forgotten, for many are the cowards of this world."

And the Wallwave answered the Bullaxe, "Then let me take the place of my good uncle. May I be sacrificed for family honor. May I be headcut in the place of the Summersailor. So you cut off my head, for he has cut off yours, though that has seemed to do you little harm. So cut my head off and avenge yourself in justice or in honest fun and games."

Then Bullaxe laughed and roared in hilarity. "Yes, let me find a fair and honest bargain. When you lie down and I cut off your head, you will be in the place of Summersailor. Naturally, for Fair is Fair and Tit for Tat, then you can take my head off in return."

The Wallwave lay down with his neck upon the log, submissively and mildly closing his eyes.

Bullaxe raised his axe above the head of Wallwave and brought it swiftly down with all his might upon the hand of the Truthteller who now appeared protecting the Wallwave.

Whitehair drew back and turned her head in horror but Wallwave lay there well and whole. The great palace roared a shout of triumph as the Wallwave rose up to his feet and bowed to Truthteller, master of good words, the godfather of Wallwave of the waves.

Truthteller blew the dust from his strong hand. Tall, gray, distinguished and dressed in modest tunic with a great sheaf of darts, all words of truth. Erect and old and powerful, a king of stars. Truthteller, the great hunter of the universe.

Then Truthteller took his sheaf of crossbow darts and shook those silver bolts ready to use them and shoot them into the heart of any liar.

Bullaxe bowed low to the tall and erect Truthteller and mumbled, "I had no right to take the head of Wallwave, in place of Summersailor."

Then, addressing the Wallwave, Bullaxe cried, "You have passed my test in courage and in truth and honor but not in skill and strength. Let's see if you are strong and skilled enough to behead me. Ha, ha, ha. Let's play my little game of Tit for Tat and Head for Head, in turn. For you must pass in skill as well as in guts and truth."

Bullaxe handed his mighty axe to Wallwave. Then he lay facedown with his neck upon the log and in quiet cheerfulness he closed his eyes.

Wallwave took hold of the massive axe with ease and raised it high above the neck of Bullaxe. Then he severed the head sharply from its body. The head rolled over on the floor and bled great clots of blood from eyes and ears and nose and from its severed butt.

In agony the head of Bullaxe swore vengeance. But the Wallwave drew his strength and struck the head again until it silenced under the blows and fell into small pieces. The crushing blows of the great axe was like the wind as it cut through branches of great trees, tempest tossed in a might of rattling storm.

Nevertheless, Bullaxe stood up again and gathered the pieces of his head even as they bled and, seizing back his axe, stalked to the doorway laughing and a-murmuring in a deep mutter.

"You have passed, Wallwave, in courage and in honor and now in skill," muttered the fragments of the severed head.

Bullaxe strode out of the doorway holding his head, fitted together from its several pieces.

The dignified Truthteller, tall in his eternal strength and power, followed after the Bullaxe. The great Truthteller of the universe, the king of good wisdom, held the true-word bolts for his crossbow as he walked beside the mutilated monster from the swamp, who was bleeding and groaning from his cruel beheading.

As they strode away from the great gate of the palace, Truthteller shot a flash of flying darts from his great crossbow, winging across the sky. All deadly shots of truths from his sure hand, piercing the throats of random liars, speaking all over the world and choking them to death.

Then Truthteller flew to his secret home in the sky.

The ugly oaf, Bullaxe, plodded on. Still lumbering, he changed back into a bushy treetrunk as he sank into his bog and disappeared.

***

Wallwave was welcomed by the other warriors and by his cousin Whitehair whom he loved and to whom he was engaged.

She asked Wallwave, "How could you have laid down in the way you did? If Truthteller had not saved you, you would have died. And we would have lost a king, a challenger to Warchariot and all his bands of liars, landthieves and assassins. We would have had no warrior to avenge the cunning playact of your father's death. We would have had no champion to prevent a thousand other such dramas and deadly cold rehearsals to take the lives of many."

Wallwave took the lovely hand of Whitehair and kissed it. "My dear cousin, if it is my destiny to avenge the death of my father, I knew I would not die. If it should not so be my destiny, then I would just as soon have died there on that log, as my head rolled, for life would not be good without my honor. Now I am sure that my true destiny is to avenge my father's cunning murder to make a place for many to dwell in peace."

At these words dread fell on the assembly, for they knew that horrible wars would follow on. Yet all raised up their swords and saluted Wallwave as the supreme king of the Wavewarriors and first in skill and courage and in honor.

Then Wallwave went back to his ship and sailed away. Back into the eastern wilderness of the seakings to seek the truth of good for true victory, to plan for the turmoil and the wars ahead, to parley with the princes who would help him.

CHAPTER SIX
THE WITCHES BREW

Then Wallwave sent out his birds of message to all his armies and his champions and supporters and all who paid their homage to his kingship. The word was sent out that Wallwave was in mourning.

The witches of water and air and earth and fire from the four corners of the earth came together and their names were: Windweasel, Rivershark, Landslink and Meteoreyes. These four witches took over a great deserted hostelry that was known as the Inn of Warwords.

Balconies were raised for the seating of the heroes, and strewn with rushes and flowers and herbs and leaves for both the Wavewarriors and the Hillwolves. These balconies were held up by strong granite, in the form of fine carved pillars studded with gems and around the balconies were walls of glass for the viewing of the comings and goings from the castle. Gold, silver and bronze jewels were on the posts.

Over the front door there was raised up, higher than the balconies of the champions and heroes, a huge sun-room also covered in glass for the four witches. This large and elegant balcony was also studded with carbuncles and precious gems of diamond and ruby, moonstone and pearl and amethyst so that it shone as brightly in the night as in the day.

All the balconies were furnished with couches, beds and pillows and quilts. Tables were set up of breads and cakes and fruits and all the finest of cooked and salted porks, muttons and beef and wild fish of the deep. Caldrons and vats of ale and wines were there, all for the serving girls to bring to table in cups or plates of gleaming gold and silver.

Lyrics, ballads and tales were also to be sung and played by the songwriters, singers and storytellers.

The four witches: Windweasel, Rivershark, Landslink and Meteoreyes, began to work their magic. The wrinkled, wizened and gaunt old crones plotted together. These vile daughters of the grave were now kept alive only by spells and magic artifacts that strike against all truth and natural vision.

"So, let us set up this Hall of Warwords in order to entertain all the Wavewarriors and their enemies, the Hillwolves," said Landslink. "An Inn of supposed peace but really a place where words of war prevail. Let us find ways to bring about confusion among the Wavewarriors now that they have no leader. For now the Wallwave is far off and dreams of wisdom."

Windweasel clutched and then unclutched the air with her sharp wrinkled claws and sneered her toothless mouth, "Let us send out our many-colored message birds to lure the Wavewarriors to a war of words.

"So we will unleash the hounds of wicked words and set them on the foe, the Wavewarriors, who will be torn apart like lambs by foxes. For nothing is as dangerous as a dangerous word. Let us also ban the use of every weapon, except for women's weapons of self-protection, and keep the men's weapons under guard until they leave our house of hospitality."

Rivershark agreed with warted lips and thinly sniggered and wiped away her dribble, "Then let both sides also give their word of honor, their pledge not to attack each other. To lay no hand or weapon upon each other until they leave these walls."

"Let us now," cried Meteoreyes: whose eyes were burning flames: whose head was bald as stone: whose mouth was toothless, "call up a spellmist all around, so that no one will hate us or despise us, so that no one will know us as we are. For if they saw our ugliness or smelt the filth of our great ages, as of the grave, or heard our bones creak and our voices hoarsen or touched our warted, loose and withered skin, they would not trust us to give good advice."

"Agreed," Windweasel croaked and hid her face. "Let all who see us, see us in great beauty and smell the lavender of summer days and hear the soft voices of the whispering nymph, taste the soft kisses of the smoothest skin and touch the hands of kindliest devotion. Let us be whitewashed tombs who will allure the living into the halls of festering death and beckon the young into the fetid pit. Let these illusions all be brought about by the aromas of the flowers of evil."

Then withering and dying flowers appeared before them with putrefying snakes crawling and festering. The smell of sweet death rose up as the flowers melted into one mass of poisonous delusion.

But the powers of the witches had their strict bounds and limits, as the Meteoreyes pointed out to the other witches.

"Yes, all this smell of illusion is created only to link up with the dreams of men who seek for ladyloves. For them the dream will appear to be reality. But all the young girls and the ladies who would come as guests will not be fooled or illusioned by the spellmist. For we are the queens of chimera creation and hallucination."

Landslink agreed with all these boastful words of snare and the spiderlair of miragecraft, "We will have food and wine to lure them in and once inside we will control the warwords.

"Alas Wallwave, the king of all the Wavewarriors, will not be here to suffer darts of warwords and so become unsettled and confused, for now he hides and mourns in far, deep waters."

And the Windweasel replied, "That is unfortunate. For now the Wallwave enjoys the help of gods and how often can the gods permit such miracles once he is compromised in skill or honor?"

"Yes, true," replied the Rivershark, "we need to find a chink in all his goodboy armor and we'll not find it while he dwells far off."

"Later," Windweasel agreed, "his time will come when we, as carrion crows, patrol the war fields in search of bodies of dead and vile, decaying bones to make our meals.

"Only because the Wallwave is in the right, his father murdered, can such a thing as help from on high be possible?   Look at all history and see how few the times that the masters of fate ever rescue a man from man's destruction. Rarely, if ever. Wallwave is no icon. Soon he will make mistakes. Aye, worse than mistakes. He will do wrong; then must his godfather desert him. Then in our fury we will seize him and try our deadly witchcraft on his thoughts and spread before him all our mind delusion."

The four browned hags, four crones of bones and wrinkles, ancient and shriveled up, trembled their claws. They shook in fear of the magic come upon them. Wraithly witches in white rags they shimmered and undulated in a strange spellmist.

Then Windweasel leered, a vile sharpminded crone with deep lines running from her withered cheekbones to her thick-warted mouth. Her skin was dry and hard like battered leather. Her eyes were deepset, piercing, darkly knowing, and cruelwise, a crone of cunning, her arthritic bony body was groaning and moaning and hurting as she spoke, croaking and whispering out her words of deceit, "Let us entrap them with this spell of flowers."

Then all were seen in a light hazy mist like women in their prime of health and loveliness. Yet they still dwelt in homes of foulest torment; for the darkest torture chamber is the body of old age as it mourns and moans and aches.

To make the slightest movement, even to breathe, is like torture creeping slowly upon the body inflicted by the knives of a cruel enemy. The screw of heart, the claws of lungs and spine.

Truly, old age is a rack of dying torment and a torture chamber that groans and creaks and reeks. Fortunate are the dead heroes who evade it.

Then the witches let fly out the birds of message, to change into the form of singing damsels. They sang out invitations to the castle, inviting both the Wavewarriors and Hillwolves, to come to bathe and eat and drink and listen in the hospitality of the queens of peace as the vile hags had falsely called themselves.

So the servile invitations had gone out, to the sweet music of the moon, to come and relax and listen to tales of olden, golden battles. Yes, to listen to the tales of wars gone by.

The warriors who received the messages replied, "Yes, we will come if our own songwriters and musicians and our singers also come with us to tell our versions of the tales of war."

Then the maids and messengers transformed back into gulls and flew away to the Castle of Warwords. A place of drinking horns, both large and small, and leather water bottles and cups and dishes. A mouth-delightful place of wines and honeys. There a beautiful and sumptuous meal was prepared with beef and pork and beer for every champion and fit for the nobles of both the Wavewarriors and the Wolves.

The storytellers and singers and reciters of poems and dancers and acrobats were all gathered in to play their harps and strings and pipes and accordions, kettledrums and whistles were tapping and clapping, great drums and little drums and also tambourines.

The walls were decked with mighty wooden shields transfixed with bosses of bright shining steel to symbolize protection and hospitality. The shields were all circumferenced with silken quivering fringes of coolest blue. These tassels shook and moaned.

Among these shields of warning and protection there hung the magic shield of battle warning. High on its watchful wall with eyes and ears, fingers and noses and silent mouths of spying, there hung the Shield of Roar, greatest of shields. It gave a mighty roar, this Shield of Roar, to warn of danger coming to a true warrior. This voice varied depending on the hazard. Like the sensitive hairs in an ear that listens quietly to the sounds and murmurings and rustles of an enemy, the Shield of Roar hears the secret whisperings of conspiracy then groans in fear that sudden death is near. This was to be the prize for the best champion, a shieldshare friend for warnings in good time.

In the halls of banqueting and the rooms of rest, the walls of red yew had smoothest copper trimmings. The champions' rooms were faced with bronze and silver and golden birds looked down from the high ceilings with precious gems for eyes.

In one dark corner there trembled a silver apple tree and on it there grew three apples of the finest gold. When dangerous words were spoken, the tree shook and all who saw fell silent, not to unleash the deathblows following on a war of words.

In the arsenal, where the warriors left their weapons, there stood the Bonespear, made from the dead bones of champions and water monsters found upon the beach, long and well balanced and deadly sharp, a flyer. This spear was red and dealt out poisoned blood when it struck a foe, the poison of dead men spurted into any enemy whom it struck. When the Bonespear was a long time lying idle it craved for blood and death, burst into flames and screamed for enemies. It had to be plunged into a vat of red wine to quench its thirst for death and terror. Otherwise the spear would kill its owner to satiate its blood lust.

So the old witches gave the spear its wine, its bloodred wine to satiate it and let the Bonespear serve out its drinks of death and so appease its appetite as it flew out over the clouds of war to its death destiny.

The Bonespear was to be given as a prize to the Wavechampion at the battle of warwords.

There also stood the quivering Rainbowsword called Hardblade. This sword was to be won by the Hillchampion of the warwords to be judged by the witches: Windweasel, Rivershark, Landslink and Meteoreyes. This magic sword, when it was waved, could draw a rainbow in the sky, a moving circle of color that would call upon the warriors to look and see the wonders of the battle.

This sword had a hilt of silver ornaments. When the tip of the sword was bent back to the hilt, it sprang back to its full length as straight as before. As flexible as a dagger, sharp as any razor, fit to split in two a leaf on the river, fit to cut a hair in two on a man's head without touching his skin. And fit to slice a man into two parts from head to hips without his realizing it for some time afterwards, each half not missing the other half at once when he would fall into two halves, stunned and stultified and having felt no pain, so swift the slice.

And in the trophy room of the Castle of Warwords, there was set out a museum of the heads of fallen heroes. And there stood all the weapons of the dead heroes, the swords and shields and spears of the oldtime greatones of the Hillwolves and the Wavewarriors. This was also a reminder of ancient allegiances and tribal trusts, faded alliances and tales of wars now dim and half forgotten.

There also were displayed the present weapons of those who visited, as a safeguard against drinking and arguing and mutual threatenings, which lead to instant fights and vicious duels. For all were under a pledge of peace and bound to keep real fights and killings to some time later, outside the walls of wartalk and long feasting. The brightness of the sun flashed on the hilts of all the swords and the rings and bands of silver and gold around them.

There also were drinking horns and goblets of white silver for the champions to drink their mead and strong red wine before the blazing fires of logs and tinder. For the air is cold and damp inside the castle although no wind or rains are blowing there.

Chill is the color of killing.

CHAPTER SEVEN
GUESTS ARRIVE

The four witches went up to the parapet and looked across the plains. There in the distance they saw four chariots coming and behind those chariots clouds of dust as of many men at arms.

Windweasel shaded her eyes from the sun as she watched the approaching chariots of the Wavewarriors. Then she called for a servant girl, "Come here young woman, your eyes are fresh, look over the plain and tell us whatever you can see, in greatest detail, coming upon us from the northern ice."

The servant girl called out the things she saw. "I see the first of four great chariots, gleaming of gold and silver in the sun. It is drawn by two huge seahorses of grey foam. This lovely chariot is drawn by the two grey dappled, galloping in time together, at one speed and pace. Their ears are pricked and both their heads held high, snorting and fuming from their broad nostrils in the heat of gallop. Those horses are lean and hard, muscular in the legs and sides but broad in chests and foreheads as they prance proudly with curled tails and manes. They pull ahead of the other three great chariots and draw more close to us. Around the chariot there floats a mist of herolight, a halo.

"Inside the chariot are four girls of beauty and, sitting on their knees, three gangling birds with lean and bony legs and flapping wings. The bird necks are bent and long and thin. Each bird has a large and drooping bill that speaks out words."

Then Rivershark spoke to the other witches, "Those are the three message cranes of the Wallwave, who scan and search the skies for a forewarning." And then she asked the young clear-sighted girl, "Tell me. Is there a warrior in the chariot?"

The girl looked out to the plain and then replied. "No, only fine ladies of great breeding and beauty all dressed like warriorwomen of the Seagulls."

Landslink thought for a moment and then addressed the other witches, "Those ladies must be Whitehair, the niece of Summersailor and her three high-born princesses in waiting.

"See, she enjoys the trust of the three birds. For even now, Whitehair throws high in the air the three fine message birds of the Wallwave and each one flies around the other chariots. There, one cries, 'Do not come, no, do not come' while another screeches out, 'Go past the castle.' Again, 'Go past the castle' and the third crane screams at the third following chariot, 'Get away.' Again it screams out, 'Danger, get away' but still the chariots continue coming towards us."

"Ah, good," cried Meteoreyes, as the witches chortled, "they are coming towards us, inexorably strong, despite all the warnings, they are coming to us and we must welcome them with open arms. See how the cranes of warning flap their wings and, leaning forward into the air, fly back to rejoin Whitehair in the Wallwave's chariot along with her three ladies-in-waiting: Maplewine, Willowflame and Streamflower. Her chariot stops on the plain and does not approach. It lies in wait, perhaps for other chariots to join it. The other three great chariots are still coming."

Then Rivershark cried out, "What is that roar, that muttering turbulence, that growling echo? Never before have I heard such rumbling thunder, with no clouds in the sky, on a sunny day with only a hum of bees.

"See, some of the weapons on our walls fall down. Some impaled skulls begin to shake their heads; the heads shake up and down, dead-eyed and dusty. No, no, they say and then change their mind and nod. Slowly and sinisterly they do agree.

"Anyhow, let us get back to looking at the guests. Now speak on, servant girl and tell us further what can you see?"

"I see a great division of fighting men in chariots with spears and swords, bosses of shields, all gleaming in the sun. At their head, in a mighty chariot, two powerful champions of war covered with strange and speckled feathers. Those men who drive it hold fivepronged javelins and broadshields trimmed with gold and gold-trimmed also are their purple tunics. This glittering host are Wavewarriors from the sea, to judge by their seabird feathers and green seaweed, their reddish yellow hair and long forked beards. Now, as they drive closer, I think I see that their chariot is built of fine yew tree and wicker, all polished up like new. The yoke is curved with silver embellishments. The wheels are of black iron. The yellow reins are soft but flexible . . ."

Then Rivershark muttered to the other witches, "Those in that coming chariot are brothers, Whaleroarer and Stormleaper of the Seawarriors.

"They are heroes of many battles, twin storms of war, two flames of judgment, knives of victory, who easily could slash the foe to pieces. Their flying swords in battle cut through men as a butcher's kitchen knife can cut through pork. The backstroke of their swords is like the wave as it leaves the shore, strong and inflexible. In their wrath and killfury they can cut down foes like the keen scythes of chariot wheels through corn. If they come here we must entrap their minds."

"Yes it is so. We must put spells upon them," agreed Windweasel, "but Whitehair is the Queen of Willowflame, Maplewine and the Streamflower, they are her ladies and her friends in waiting. They have hopes of winning heroes. But Whitehair is the one of whom we must beware for she is promised to the Wallwave, king of the Wavewarriors. He is the swordswift champion of the Seagulls whose courage, skills and honor have all been proven in his encounter with Bullaxe, the ogre.

"Wallwave is the most magical of the Seagulls, born under the gaze of an earthquake and the sun, in the full oversight of whitefoam ocean. He is a Wavewall of winged, icy skill, a deadly mariner of sky, earth and sea. What a pity he is in mourning for his father and cannot come to join our hospitality."

Then Landslink, Meteoreyes and the Rivershark agreed and chortled, clawing their hoods around them, "If the Wallwave would come to join his men he would be a hero worthy of our attention."

"Dear ladies," cried the girl, "I see another chariot as beautiful as the first two holding a powerful hero as they come flying over the plain."

"What does this hero's chariot look like? As it draws closer, can you see in detail?"

"On one side of the chariot's harness-pole there strides a red horse, prancing high and powerfully over the riverbanks and fields and ravines. It kicks up foaming water from the fords and hollows like swift birds flying faster than the eye. On the other side of the pole, a great black horse goes galloping at full speed over the plains, over the stones and rocky places and tree stubs.

"These two magnificent horses are pulling a chariot of fine white-polished wood with a wicker canopy covered with the feathers of wild birds. It is balanced upon two wheels of burning bronze, high set and light, creaking from side to side as it flies across the fields and narrow roads. Its central pole shines bright with silver sunlight. Its yoke is curved and smooth with yellow reins.

"In this great chariot stands a straight tall man. His skin is yellow; his eyes are gray as sky. His cheeks are red as blood, his brows are gray and in his hand he holds a long thin spear. His hair is long and wavy-white as snow. His tunic is purple and blue and on his sleeve there shows the red cuffs of a nobleman. His cloak is of white silk. A shield of brown, with boss of flowing bronze, gleams on his arm. Across his chest there hangs a waterhorn. His face is grim and lined. Stern are his eyes.

Fierce, haughty and contemptuous is his frown. His nose is high and hooked and from his nostrils there pours a steady stream of fire and flame. "

"I recognize this description," cried out Windweasel. "His frown is like the growling of a tiger. His sneer is a flame that could cut through sharpened stone. That man is the Icedragon, swift and hard and merciless to his foes. Icedragon is the third greatest of the Wavewarriors next to Wallwave and the Summersailor, the uncle of Wallwave.

"In battle after battle he has fought, heaping the heads of enemies upon heads, leaping, tumbling and twisting his sword on high. Then he twists and rolls and crawls out, jumping up high to catch his sword in midair, then lops off the heads of those who had surrounded him. Woe to the foes who charge him from behind as the Icedragon piles up heads the way a baker piles up his loaves newly baked from the oven. He is a baker from the Board of Slice, as the strange birds from the otherworld fly overhead and the fearsome herolight flashes around him, a halo given only to the chosen.

"Tell me who else do you see with your young eyes?"

"I see another warrior proud and arrogant, a mighty man of war, stout and broadstocky, mature in years, yet fit and strong and upright. Across his chest there hangs a waterhorn. No doubt it is filled with clear spring water, for he stands like one well used to giving orders, a grizzled man of grey hairs and grey beard. He glowers from a kingly chariot of redwood under a polished wicker canopy, leaning against a gleaming silver pole, embellished with bronze ornaments and gold, as his chariot rolls fiercely towards us on iron wheels."

Then Meteoreyes gazed down with better eyesight as she saw the chariot come close and enter the Castle of Warwords, the frogpool of witches spells. "That is the uncle of Wallwave, Summersailor, the viceking, now in charge of the crack division of the Wavewarriors. That chariot has a finely balanced frame. It is laced with iron made by a master craftsman for strength. Its yoke is overlaid with gold.

"The two horses are driven with yellow reins soft and gentle but yet strongest rope. Both horses are alike in size and fiery beauty; both prance and step up high in joy and speed like mistyghosts over the hard greensward or like twin hinds leaping out of the hill like two great hares jumping in the spring or like keen winter winds cutting over the plains. Their ears are pricked and sharp, their heads held high, powerful fierce nostrils breathing fire and smoke and leaping in unison magnificent. Their manes and tails are clean and curly soft. Their foreheads broad, fine eyes set well apart. Two proud high-stepping horses. One in courage, one in nobility, well bred and beautiful with sturdy legs that eagerly leap along and pound like thunder.

"Those two chariot horses, a white and a brown, throwing up sods of earth, high in the sky like birds flying out of a bush when the hunter strikes. Great is the pomp and pride of those brave horses as their tails and manes shake out and toss and shine in the broad sunlight. Their hooves are fierce and gallop and clip and echo. Their sides are tight and muscular. Their backs are broad, yet they are balanced and sure of foot.

"Smoke fumes out of their bridled mouth and nostrils in straight streams of hot air. Their legs are splashed with water and riverfoam for in their haughty spirits they have just been kicking up water from the rivers. Like a spray of meteorites they fly in joy casting aside all tiredness, snorting in triumph. I know and see these things from my foresight and knowledge."

CHAPTER EIGHT
SPELLS AND SPIDERLAIRS

The war was stirred along by the four Witches of Kill who cast their spells of delusion on the Wavewarriors so that they would be defeated by the Wolves. The three old witches were well pleased with Meteoreyes.

"We thank you, Meteoreyes, for your clear vision but what is that great cloud upon the horizon, approaching behind the chariot of Summersailor? So inexorably it seems to drive upon us."

Meteoreyes answered the other witches, "That is a great band of charioteers that stomps and strides in unison upon us like a great phalanx, well structured and in time. They swing their arms with swords and spears and javelins, hand next to hand, arm next to arm, they drive, shoulder aligned to shoulder, side by side. Each wears the cuff of nobles on his sleeve, purple and blue and red. Their coats and hoods are factored of the toughest mail. Their axes and javelins and arrows gleam in the sunlight. Wheel turning with precision next to wheel, axel lined up with axel, all as one.

"Horses come proudly towards us, like a wave of thunder on the hoof, like a great deluge of mist from the faroff sea, lit up by the lightning of spears and swords bright flashing in the sunlight. There every warrior seems to be a king in their inexorable strength and courage. They come like waves hard-driven by the storm but their strong hooves are cutting the earth so deeply that the soil is crumbling and shifting like an earthquake."

Rivershark was worried by the sight; asking the others, "What is this wave of fear? Dear ladies, what is this fearsome cloud of heroes?"

And Meteoreyes replied, "This is the Hawkarmy of Summersailor, given to him by the late king. This is the group of warriors we most fear; for no man in the world can stand before them. But we will do so. Bring the tubs of water, tables of food and casks of finest ale."

Then the tables of hospitality were set up. And the steam hissed from the tubs of icecold water as the heroes cooled their heat and calmed their minds. The heroes of the Wavewarriors were wined and given many fruits and meats to eat. The four old witches in their disguise of beauty welcomed the four heroes of the Wavewarriors: the Summersailor, Icedragon, Whaleroarer and the Stormleaper. And each fiend-witch presented to each champion a golden cup of wartriumph that claimed each hero was the conqueror of them all. And so they sowed the seeds of jealousy.

The witches bowed as Whitehair approached.

Landslink muttered to the other witches, "Show no surprise or anger as they breathe in the airs of our enchantment. The men will see us as they wish to see us but the womenfolk will see us as we are."

"Isn't it always so?" murmured the Rivershark, "but let us arrange these things as best we can. Send out to speed the secret coming of the Wolves. Let the Wolves slip in through the dark portals of night, unseen and invisibly crawling and slinking through the back doors of the basement in the castle.

"Their presence will unnerve and surprise the Seagulls. Soon we will have the Seagulls broken up for they are not expecting to meet Hillwolves.

But do not permit Warchariot to come for he and his Queen who treacheried Waterbear, and so murdered the father of Wallwave, may well become a target of revenge.

"But Flyingbat and Cragfox and our other Hillwolf heroes such as Oakhill, Winterwarrior or Ratrunner may well engage the Wavewarriors in fighting talk. So they could help to lay the foundations of bad feelings and resentments and hasty battles or traps or ambushes sometime in the days ahead. For the bloodiest of bloody wars begins with words."

Then Whitehair and her serene band of ladies entered the hall and looked around in horror to see the heroes of the Wavewarriors consort with withered hags of ugliness. They saw at once that the four Witches of Kill had foulest smelling warts and wrinkled skins with vile diseases deadlier than the plague. For what is worse than to die old and cold?

Outside the hostelry everything looked well. The sight was beautiful and a pleasure to the eye. There were fine horses, chariots, mighty men at helm. There were hundreds following far away, true men of war, a-marching over the fields, all strictly striding behind their battle leader, wearing green and yellow cuffs of poor footmen. Fine warriors but with heads held low and humble, as those of lower rank with hoods and mail, holding firm to their axes, arrows, darts and javelins ready to pass these weapons to their leaders. For those leaders had long since learned the subtleties of combat and they had greater skills of war to use a fast supply of armory to fight the foe and overwhelm the enemy.

War Queen Whitehair entered and cried out to the four heroes of the Wavewarriors: Whaleroarer, Icedragon,

Stormleaper and the Summersailor, "Think of your foot soldiers. See that they get food and why do you sojourn here at the Castle of Warwords?"

And they replied, "We wait upon our leader who is in mourning for his murdered father."

"And so you eat and drink with these four witches in this hostelry of hatred and backbiting. I have come here to protect you with my ladies-in-waiting: Willowflame and Streamflower and Maplewine. We are armed and trained as warriorwomen with swords and shields and helmets, javelins and dirks to act as witnesses in any dispute. I am here to act for the Wallwave.

"I tell you, you all must wait for the instructions of Wallwave. The stirrings and rumors and preparations for war and these grim gatherings of many forces was all because his father King Waterbear was murdered bloodily and in treachery and in lies."

Summersailor replied disdainfully, "Now it is for the Wallwave to say where we must go and when and why and how and for what purpose. Revenge or retribution towards making good all our lost ways of life and laws and justices. These matters are for the Wallwave to decide and not you, Whitehair."

"Just so my uncle but why do you eat and drink and dally with such old hags of wicked and malicious and murderous intent? For those illusions are a mere screen to hide these Witches of Kill."

The champions replied, "Leave us to rest. One woman should never try to judge another. These lovely ladies are most kind and attentive."

And the Wavewarriors laughed and sang and drank and held up their fine golden cups of champions as Whitehair cried, "Fools, you are drunk and blind for here in the air are mists and wisps of spells that breathe delusion. Don't tell me you cannot see that these ugly crones have wrought a spell upon you of sweet-smelling and enchantment?"

"Yes, Yes," the men laughed out in high amusement. "We are spellbound and enchanted with sweet smells and sweeter smiles and gentle hands to serve us, from all our welcomers of such great beauty. Look at these lovely dresses."

"Yes, they at least are real. You men are very easy to please, easy to delude and fool and easily flattered."

So Whitehair with her loyal band of ladies: Willowflame, Maplewine and the Streamflower visited back and forth from their own quarters to keep the Summersailor and the other heroes away from the close attentions of the witches.

The witches continued to loudly talk of their love of peace.

"Our mission is for a time of peace and play. The Waterbear has been most vilely murdered, but let not war break out between the two sides. No, rather let us talk and dine together at our expense. We have experience of the ways of peace."

Whitehair looked down from the stairs at the old crones and cried out, "You surely have experience of wicked wiles and war and more than all of us."

***

There is a landscape of dreams and fantasy where shades and shadows shift from mind to mind.

Strange voices and calm walkers come and go from past to present-time and to the future. Then they stalk back into the sleeping mind, with gifts of visions and with clear understandings, bringing their messages of hopes and fears. Some tread in truth, some in untruth and delusion. Only the few long practiced mind-travelers can call upon these spirits to emerge with foresights.

So the four witches went to the great waterfall for the words of the water demons and for their welcoming voices. Galegrowl to lure into a watery lair, Lakelap to cover up the floating dead and Watertrap who lies in wait and surges in gentle swirls upon the surface, hiding a deep whirlpool of darkness underneath.

The Riverroar with the hoarse voice: the Rushbreeze who is like the wind that blows through the water rushes: Seacry and Waveweep of the cool calls, the languid, liquid breeze murmurers: Stormscream, who breaks out upon the air in a surprise of sudden helpless yells: Squallwhimper and the sighing of the demons of the waterfall.

Such voices fell upon the witches' ears and drift-directed their thoughts into hazed dreams where the ghosts of the forebears of the great warriors flourished; where waters gave rise to rivers and tidal streams and the fire flared up into volcanoes and meteors. There, earth slipped around into landslides and earthquakes and air swirled out into tornadoes and storms.

Yet in the fullness of time, over the years, each of these voices would become a spiritwarrior armed to the teeth with swords and shields and armor and spears and drinking horns and javelins. Then there arose one warrior to combat all, the Wallwave, one man yet greater than all others combined.

The witches summoned up the spirit voices and told them, "Lie in your lair to call upon the Wallwave when he comes that you may deceive him and destroy him."

So the four witches laughed and spoke of peace with callous cunning and hypocrisy, "We have experience of war and hate it, for war is what destroys a land and burns up people and their food and homes.

"Later, we will bring in the heroes of the Hillwolves to talk and to be peaceable to the Wavewarriors so that we can learn to live together and to work towards a time of peace and play, a time to tell of days in the summer sun.

"All weapons will be kept locked in the armory. So let us test and try our common humanity and not our ability to curb, cut and kill, not our ability to destroy each others' lives. Let us walk down the green-flowered paths of peace.

"For when we get to know and understand that our enemies are persons and individuals, very much like ourselves, with skills and hopes and fine ambitions to plant and build the world into a better place, for our children and children's children, then we will never tread again the rocky road of war or pestilence or sad destruction.

"We need to understand that everyone who brings upon us hunger, drought and pestilence whatever side he fights for will be destroyed by such crass enmity."

CHAPTER NINE
VOICES – FALSE AND TRUE

So the witches listened to the babbling of the spirit voices in the waterfall and then talked of peace and reconciliation to the warriors gathered around in the hostelry.

But when the four witches drew aside to talk, each to the other, they sang a different song; a harsh and discordant and deathstirring melody.

So Meteoreyes addressed the other witches, "In this way the two sides can engage each other in a war of words that surely can only lead to a war of blood and death to the Wavewarriors.

"We must plot and plan sure death to the arrogant powers of these Wavewarriors who follow light and truth. They are stiff and inflexible and predictable.

"All our unexpected trickery and the force of our fierce hatred and destructiveness, our dedication and unexpectedness, in the long run must always win the day. That is why they call us Powers of Win.

"Though Whitehair and her three ladies-in-waiting are now in their quiet quarters, yet their sharp eyes are forever watching us. So let us avoid them and their magic stare, for their thoughts are always cool and calculating and come together in such a way as to tell what well might be, the ways things are slow-creeping."

And, at this time, Whitehair was telling her three ladies-in-waiting, "You need to know what spells and cunning are snaking and coiling together to come against us. For through the back and shadowy entrances of this fortress of Warwords, the four great heroes of the Hillwolves, next to Warchariot, are being smuggled into the dungeons of the castle. These are the masters of secret, unknowable illusions practiced in deceit and lies and deception; a rabble of spies, liars and saboteurs, of creators of fires that cause confusion and chaos.

"They pose as pilgrims on a godly journey or dance like cheerful, tuneful troubadours. But they are all more deadly than they seem, for their hollow trekking staffs or flutes are filled with death and conceal long stilettos of silent backstabbing or metal chains of war. Sometimes their staffs or flutes are false blowpipes for shooting out small poisoned darts that kill.

"All is not what it seems. When crafty murderers, disguised as priests or merchants, men of music or silent monks, pose as good pilgrims, set out on a godly journey or dance like cheerful, tuneful, troubadours.

"But suddenly and secretly they change. At night they are clothed from head to toe in black. Out in the fields and forest they go dressed in green so that they may suddenly drop down upon an honest traveler unsuspecting. In winter weather, they will be dressed in white with gloves and facemasks of the purest wool.

"Suddenly the snow or the bushes or the night will come alive and throw itself upon the unwary traveler or the honest warrior. Then the darkness or the snow or the greenery will rake across a face an iron claw, worn on a wristband. A nest of razor stars, coated with poison, will swing upon a calm and unsuspecting face, a face to die in a paroxysm of torment as the poison from the silver stars strikes deep.

"These are the liars of assassination who come to visit victims in strange costumes, bringing the knife stiletto in hidden pockets. They carry folding ladders and long ropes, with grappling hooks, to throw upon the walls of unsuspecting victims of the mercenary.

"These slithery assassins are often paid by the next of kin or friends who stand to gain. These secret hirers of the killer crews can see before them the gold they will inherit, after the deadly executors have crawled out in green or white or black as from the meadows or snow or darkest forest.

"May the gods protect us from our friends and families. For some of the slyest killers come to dinner. They take note of the secret ways and means by which we can be stabbed to death or poisoned and reporting all the self-protection traps that we have set to block the dread intruder. And as for those they hire to murder us, even their reeds or scabbards act as a snorkel to guide the deadly fish to approach underwater through the creeks and underground sewers and pits of filth through the waterways and rivers or wavelaps and moats - long thought, but vainly, to provide protection.

"These dark assassins swim and snorkelbreathe, smuggling their fire and smoke bombs and poisoned wax in tins and wooden boxes. Such sly murderers have been known to cut off their own foot to escape from a snaptrap set to hold and capture them.

"Their muscles and their bones are flexible for they practice coordination and manipulation. Their strength is in enduring, low-key stamina, the power to lair and snare for many hours until the victim walks into their web.

"We are surrounded by such crafty killers. These are the spidery men who have slunk in and been disarmed of swords, daggers and javelins, for all their weapons were taken to the armory. But only their fear of the witches keeps them in order, their fear of treachery and illusion and deception. So they agreed to hand over their weapons; their simple swords and spears and ropes and pulleys. For all these tools can only assassinate a few (and not the king of all, Wallwave) but lies and deceit can kill more and more thousands in days to come as men follow false visions. Later, these wolves of wartalk will speak out to undermine and to confuse the foe.

"Down in that banquet hall, right now, are lounging the greatest masters of disguise and cunning. Those wolves of danger and destruction are Cragfox and Winterwarrior and Ratrunner. The greatest liar is old Flyingbat whose brother Oakhill is a man of might and a slayer of many, though absent from the castle. Slinking where the air is cold and wet and clammy, outside the walls where the wind cuts like a knife, there lurk Oakhill and the other kings of cunning.

"Also, the regular swordfighters of the Hillwolves, cowardly but effective and deadly skilled in killing, will be led into the halls of hospitality to be wined and dined by the withered witches in their disguise of beauty. There the Hillwolves will boast of all their assassinations and provoke the great heroes of the Wavewarriors.

"So the Seafighters of the East will sit down to dine with the Hillwolves of the West. It is as though the rising suns of the eastern world were to sit down to dispute with the darkening moon. Yet, there is only a haggle of ancient crones and craggy bones, illusioning as young women, to mediate and entertain and sing for such is their delusion of youth and loveliness.

"At one great table sit the four heroes of the Wavewarriors: Icedragon, Whaleroarer, the Stormleaper and the Summersailor. These are seabreakers and seashakers, heroes all, ready with javelins, horsespirited and spearproud.

"The witches, seen as beauties, sit between them and the Hillwolves: Cragfox, Flyingbat and Ratrunner with Winterwarrior, fieldmarshal of the Wolves; he of the sudden swordbolt that transforms the living into the dead, in a twinkling eye.

"The youths and the entertainers and singers and songwriters join in the feasting and the merriment. This all is the disaster spread before us."

***

At this time, after Whitehair had told her ladies of the great dangers that nightmagic held in store for all the Seagulls, the hero Summersailor came to visit his niece in the ladies' boudoir.

"Sit down, my uncle; I have a story for you and I have a warning to give to all the Wavewarriors. Those crones, those hags, those witches are all enchanted. For they metamorphize with strange spells and smells. You see them as young and pretty but we see them as they really are, without their perfume magic."

Then Summersailor spread his hands, "We differ. All beauty is in the eye of the beholder."

"Just so, but watch that your mind is not invaded there. Down below, in the banqueting hall, you have the four most powerful witches on the earth: Windweasel, Rivershark, Landslink and Meteoreyes. Beware of their deceptions and their lies, for they will lead you all to your destruction. Avoid the Feast of Witches and Delusions. Disaster is the only place they go.

"Remember the story of the two young lovers:

"Faith, the young girl, was deeply in love with Hope. Hope loved young Faith and planned to marry her, at Charity beside the Emerald Sea. Living far, far apart they made a pact to travel to Charity and there get married. Then Hope set out and met with the four witches seeing them falsely as young girls of beauty. He asked them what news had they heard. The four witches wept and cried and mourned. Have you not yet been told the terrible news? It is a fact that Faith, the loyal one, set out to see her young true sweetheart Hope, and meet with him and marry in Charity; that the vile witches of the clouds of war prevented her and held her against her will and so Faith died of shock and a broken heart.

"The witches falsely told the young man, Hope, 'Faith is now dead, let us all mourn her passing.' And the witches wailed and wept and screamed and cried. Hope died of a broken heart when he heard the lies, falsely telling him of the death of Faith.

"Faith, at this time, was alive and preparing to go to meet with Hope. Then the witches, seen by Faith, as the true ugly ones they were in reality, came to Faith's home to visit the young girl and tell her of the death of Hope. And truly so.

"When Faith heard of the death of Hope she too fell over with a broken heart and died.

"The four witches chortled and danced in mirth and stole the body of Faith and buried it beside the body of Hope where he lay buried beside the Emerald Sea. Then an apple tree grew over both their graves.

"True lovers now go there to eat the apples and to promise never to believe the things that people tell them about each other, but to demand the proof. They promise to have faith and hope and to live in charity.

"And so I beg you uncle and viceking, avoid the company of witches. Leave them now. Let us go on our way, with the other brave Wavewarriors to meet with the Wallwave before the witches drive you to disaster. For Destruction is the only city they know."

So Whitehair ended her true tale of warning told to her uncle to save him from the wiles and treacheries of lies and mind illusion.

But Summersailor stood up and bowed to Whitehair and to her three ladies-in-waiting. "Thank you for that fine tale, a pretty fable, but not one that we need to take too seriously. The women that you speak of are not witches but kindly ladies of beauty and hospitality."

Then Summersailor left Whitehair and rejoined the Feast of Witches.

Whitehair smashed her glass down on the floor. After this she would go to see her uncle to bring him presents of fine fruit or mead. Likewise her ladies-in-waiting made frequent visits to the chief heroes of the Wavewarriors. But they kept with them their weapons of self-protection, for they were not bound under the oath of peace.

Streamflower, dressed like a true warriorwoman, in blue mail with silver sword and shield and javelin, her yellow hair flowing out beneath her helmet, would come to see Stormleaper from time to time.

Maplewine was dressed in blood-red tunic and mail, with all the accouterments of war when she gave small sweet glasses to the Whaleroarer.

Willowflame was also in combat armaments for her protection, red hair flowing down across her shoulders as she brought with her fruit and honey to Icedragon where he sat in the hall.

The heroes of the Wavewarriors were pleased and flattered to receive these small attentions, for Whitehair and her ladies were of great beauty but the witches were jealous and furious at these distractions. They turned to others, the charms of their delusions, so that many other warriors were deceived with the false beauty of the shriveled crones. And so it came about that many warriors suffered unstable tremors of the mind, and later, in their days of war and travel, were easily bewildered, dazed and scattered when all the false wining and dining had been ended.

CHAPTER TEN
UNDERCURRENTS

So it was that in the great feasting hall of couches and tables, the Seagulls and the Hillwolves sat around.

The witch Windweasel reminded all those present, "Remember you can collect your weapons and shields only when you leave this hall of feasting. Remember you are under oath and bond, upon the witness of your honorable name, to use no violence against anyone while you are here relaxing, eating and drinking. Whoever breaks his bond will be put to death by all the others. It is agreed between us. So let us have a time of peace and plenty."

Even the serving girls shrank back in fear of the ugly hags of witches, wondering why the warriors wined and dined with such skinny crones. As the men breathed in the perfumes of the witches and the smells went to their heads, their vision changed from that of hideous hags to lovely ladies.

***

Then the treacherous Ratrunner spoke to the Icedragon, "Your poor performance is well known in battle. I speak to you as a friend. What do you say?"

"Well," replied the Icedragon, "I must admit that my horses and my horsemanship are clumsy. It is well known how ponderously my chariot turns around in combat and how each chariot wheel digs a deep ditch that lies open for a year. Slowly but surely is my combat motto."

Icedragon then smiled and nodded to Ratrunner.

Ratrunner bowed and laughed, "I told you so. You are the slowest of the slow in battle and one day your clumsiness must result in death."

"Well, I cannot agree," said the Icedragon, "I have never yet been the loser in a combat and horsemanship is not the only story.

"Like a cock crowing suddenly in the cold dawn, to rise up like a bird and go to combat with the heavy harness of battle across my shoulders, I have been strong to gallop over fords and kick up a great spray against the enemy, flying into the faces of the foe in singlehanded combat, skill and fury.

"Also, I have breasted rains of flying javelins with only one great shield and a handful of spears. I have looked down upon the bones of many. And I will still practice my chariot feats in days to come before both kings and heroes.

"I will join with my great comrades of the Seagulls, shoulder to shoulder and in step by step, swords drawn and pointed towards the enemy. In harness with my comrades I will slaughter in treacherous and hard terrain, in thick woodlands, high rivers and rockhills, along the borders where foes are lying low. Nor can any hero meet me in single combat."

"Oh really, so? I will believe your boasting only when I can see it with my own eyes." Ratrunner sneered.

Icedragon laughed in scorn. "This is a strange hostelry for friendships. Yes, here there is a low breeze, an underflow of jealousy and resentment and near-hatred that lurks beneath the surface of casual manners. What kind of company is this? When I speak humbly, people will believe me and will take my word but when I speak with pride and powerful promise they disbelieve me, sneer at me and argue.

"They try to break me low and so destroy me. Make up your mind. Am I a truther or liar? Or do you just believe whatever suits you? Your own weak fantasy is far from reality."

"You are a strange one to talk of fantasy with all your boasting, bragging and arrogant bluster," said Ratrunner as he sneered at the Icedragon.

Icedragon replied, "I am content to wait until one day I meet you on a field of single combat." Then the Icedragon moved to talk to friends.

Landslink opened a small box that she had taken from the servant of Whaleroarer and cried, "A dead dog! Who has dared to bring this here? A dead dog into a house of feasting and wine. Remove this vermin rubbish from our banquet."

The Whaleroarer stepped over to his charioteer Strongherd, "This is my dog Guardhunt! How can he be dead so soon? I left him tethered, fed and content?"

"Master, Guardhunt went missing and I ran hither and thither, up and down and everywhere. I called for him, whistled and looked high and low.

"I met Cragfox and he told me, 'You'll find your dog dead on the shore,' and sure enough he lay there, all limp and wet and lifeless, drowned I think, by the hand of Cragfox, the cold killer of dogs."

"There is no need to think or speculate, good man, for here I am, Cragfox. I drowned the dog," spoke up a Hillwolf from among the crowd.

"Why?" asked Whaleroarer, "Did you murder him?"

"I did not murder it. I merely drowned it."

"And yet, you tied a stone around his neck and threw him in the sea. The tide returned and my drowned dog was thrown in on the tide?"

"Well, yes. I hope that that was not too hard on you. After all, a dog is only a mutt to us and we can find plenty more for next to nothing. So, no harm done, I believe you will agree."

Then the four witches rubbed their hands gleefully to see the Whaleroarer look so miserable. For the Whaleroarer looked like one who wore shackles of sorrow and handcuffs of misery; to be led down a path that leads to death.

Whaleroarer took the small coffin with the dead dog. "My good old dog is dead. He was my henchman. He was more faithful to me than any cousin. Dependable and fast in finding and killing deer or wild hogs. He was also stalwart in guarding our home and horses and our cattle. He was a true defense for ducks and geese.

"In our day of battle combat he stood by me. He was my friend and guard and true defender, in chariot, in duel and in the field. He guarded our good name and kept us company. He was a friend of ours, my good old dog.

But what a cold, lonely death, to die at sea."

Cragfox replied in regret to the Whaleroarer, "I was misled by one of our hostesses. The hostess with eyes of burning flame told me she had come by a report that a bad black and white shepherd dog was running rabid and terrifying the horses where the horses were on rein and could not escape. She asked me to chase the mongrel out to sea.

"I know the shoreline well with all its slick and sloping, slippery rocks, its treacherous currents, its whirlpools and drownspots. Certainly, I have often patrolled and mounted a guard upon the shoreline to keep a lookout for our enemies. I did not know the dog meant so much to you. Do please remember all this is about an animal. This whole misunderstanding is outside the bond and promise of our agreement not to engage each other in deadly combat.

Here in the hall of words, you cannot break your bond and oath over the death of a dog."

"I know it, I have no intention of it," said the Whaleroarer as he sipped his wine.

Cragfox, lean, dark, watchful, then walked out into the thin chills of the murderous night.

The Whaleroarer muttered out a curse, "May she who caused my poor dog to be drowned, one day be drowned herself in the dread sea."

Then Flyingbat, one of a family of killers who hired out to kill for gold and silver, remarked to Stormleaper of the Wavewarriors, "Cragfox, now that he has said he is sorry for the dog's death, takes the whole matter as over and done with but he is very anxious to leave nevertheless.

"For Cragfox besneaks himself out into the dark where he is at home. Few will be able to overcome him there and all because he killed a dirty dog and the dog's owner moans.

"Stormleaper, I can tell you truly and for certain who killed your father when you were a child. That is, you must agree, much more important that any killing of a mangy whelp. Wouldn't you like to know who killed your father? I heard it happened in your father's bedroom inside your fastness, windows and doors full locked."

The Stormleaper started up, "I well remember. It was a mystery. I thought it supernatural. My father was locked within his room, yet murdered."

Then Flyingbat slyly told his tale to the Stormleaper. "Oakhill, my elder brother, tells of the day he killed your father. Often Oakhill boasts about it. And perhaps that is the reason why he has not come here to talk about it. Perhaps he is too kind to cause offense.

"My elder brother has often unlocked that mystery. He tells of how he wore assassins clothes, dressed in a black suit and a mask, he crept into your fort in the dark hours when all your family were feasting.

"Hiding from the servants, Oakhill crept into the rafters above the bed in the steel room where your father normally slept. The windows and the barred door had been locked but the skillful burglar Oakhill had unlocked them. Silent and motionless Oakhill hid there clinging to the rafters and the beams until, long after dark, your father came to sleep.

"Then looking down upon your father, Oakhill stretched down his spear and held it till the dawn light filtered into the room. The weapon pointed at and almost touched your father's heart. Then Oakhill leaned on the spear and fell down hard upon it piercing the heart and tearing it apart without a single scream from your sleeping father."

Then Flyingbat continued with his tale, "I was only a boy myself when I heard of it. Yes, it seems that then Oakhill seized up the keys of the lock, lying upon the lockerbox beside the bed, he let himself out. And once outside the bars of the bedroom door he locked the door again and threw the ring of keys under the door to fall beside the bed. Then down the stairs he stole in his dark suit, his black-tarred sword and the shield in his blackened hand. He let himself out through a small cellar window.

"Later your family found your father dead, although he was locked inside his steelbuilt bedroom. Some people thought that magic had been worked. My brother Oakhill gained a fortune for this deed, paid to him by your father's enemies.

"Now we are wealthy we would do the same for you and likewise kill your family's foes or rivals for a good price.

It is our business and I have nothing against you. It's all money."

"Thank you," replied Stormleaper the Wavewarrior. "Let me just think about it for a while."

Flyingbat continued, "We would do a good job for you, if we were well paid.

"You can see that Oakhill is a cunning warrior. No one has ever been known to stand against him. He has disposed of many who were thought to be invulnerable. Oakhill has great strength as well as skill and craftiness."

"Of course and I will think it over," agreed Stormleaper.

Then Stormleaper moved away and joined the company of Summersailor, the viceking and spoke to him. And Summersailor quietly replied, "Those words were spoken only to provoke. See that you lay no hand or weapon on him. Flyingbat is a boaster. Do not break our bond and our agreement. Do not force us ever to behead you for the sake of honor."

"Please believe me Summersailor, I am attached to this poor head and I will not desert it, for it is too bowed and broken to be abandoned."

"Good man," said Summersailor, and gripped hard upon the upper arm of the Stormleaper.

Then the Stormleaper left the food and wine to walk outside into the quiet of the night.

He took his leave from viceking Summersailor with a low bow, a sad respect, a longing to linger longer, but with a need to go.

Meteoreyes decided to introduce Summersailor to Winterwarrior.

Summersailor, "Here meet your opposite from the Hillwolves, the viceking of the hills, Winterwarrior the veteran and fieldmarshal. As you may know, it is our hope to avoid a War of Kill. So, talk to the great fieldmarshal of all the divisions of the Hillwolves. Then you can talk man to man of peace and plenty."

Old Winterwarrior was most frank and friendly. He warmly shook the hand of Summersailor.

"It seems you rule the waves and we the land. This we could bear, if we could have free passage to cross the seas but if you block our way how can we avoid a conflict where too many can only lose their lives and limbs and fortunes. Come here with me and I will show you all our secret stores of wealth that could be yours if only you would join us and not murder us."

"Your king, the Warchariot, was the one who started all the murder and mayhem," said Summersailor.

"Yes," Winterwarrior agreed, most pleasantly. "Just so and I am glad you mentioned this. I had no part of that. Warchariot is cold and cruel."

Here the Winterwarrior looked around furtively, "It would be no great hardship for me to be king but I would never dare to move against him. He is too murderous. Also there is no need. One day, and soon, his enemies will destroy him. You might as well be my true righthand man as viceking to the very young Wallwave.

"Young heroes come and go but we old warriors go on forever. We are time and combat scarred. Anyway, dear fellow, let me show you something and think about what I said. Here in this basement. . ." (as they came to a large stone flight of steps and entered and passed the ten ranks of guardians and heroes) "is the greatest thing that any army can have - all you will ever need of food and gold.

"There is a cauldron always filled with wine and also large enough to hold three cows.

"There are seven cauldrons filled with salted boars, fattened and tender. Since they were small piglets they were fed on only the best of springtime meat. They drank only cow milk, curds and whey galore. In summer they ate meal: in autumn, nuts, muesli and wheat: in winter, meats and broths.

"There are seven full-sized cows a-roasting there and since they have been but calves they have been fed only on heather and twigs, fresh herbs and honey with meadow grass and corn.

"There are always baking two hundred wheat cakes, cooked in purest honey from fifty bushels of wheat so that each bushel makes just four cakes.

"And there is a pile of gold, right in the center, as large as three good pigs. My crack division needs a rich supply of living gold and food for fighting, as you can see, in order to keep my men going like heroes and you deserve no less for your Hawkarmy. Where else in all the world could you get this? Here, take a small sample of this gold to test it."

Summersailor lifted up a piece of gold, appraised it, held it up to catch the light, nodded in appreciation and acceptance and put it in his pouch.

Then Winterwarrior, fieldmarshal of the Wolves and Summersailor went back to join the feasting.

Meteoreyes was eavesdropping on their conversation. She spoke once more to Winterwarrior and led him to the hall, "Let us just stand aside and say no more. What you have said to the Summersailor was truly said with words of great persuasion."

As the day dusked, the hardblade Rainbowsword was seized by the Summersailor as his prize and no one on either side dared challenge him.

Then the feasting went on long into the night. As they sat there, the young serving girls carried the drinking horns and cups of silver and gold, studded with stone-brights. Strong drink was set up and choicest meats and fish and varied fruits.

The young were merry. Courage and calmness rose up within the fighting men. The women were full of gentleness and kindness serving.

Yet, the feast was misted over with mindmadness and a haze of dim delusion shadowed the singers. In the words of the songwriters and singers were knowledge and foreknowledge.

So the malice-talk and the word-wounding did not end until the sunrise dawned on another day.

CHAPTER ELEVEN
SCATTERING OF THE SEAGULLS

Then Summersailor rose up at dawn, like the cock that struts and scans at the screech of the day. A herolight shone all about the warrior and a halo of fire and brightness flashed around him as he leapt out to greet his crack division, the great Hawkarmy, best of the Wavewarriors.

He gave the cry, "Hawkrise," and they rose up, ready for a demonstration of their skills.

Then Summersailor unsheathed his Rainbowsword, swung it around and drew a rainbow, high in the sky above. As the dawn streaked over the sky in grey and light blue, many of the people sat up to see the Hawkarmy arising.

The display of arms was watched by other divisions of the Wavewarriors: the sleepers in the castle and the Hillwolves camping further off: the witches: the songwriters: the rabble of foodsellers: gossips: the storytellers and campfollowers.

The Hawk charioteers rose up and seized the tackle and harnessed it on the stallions. Great was the pomp and pride of those brave horses, as their tails and manes shook out and shone and tossed.

Then the Hawkwarriors spread their wings of war and jumped into their chariots fully armed with their swords and shields, their javelins and daggers, axes and bows and arrows and slingstones.

All shoulder to shoulder, and in step by step, their weapons pointed at each others throats. They all disarmed each other of their swords, seizing the sword of the other with their lefthands.

Each warrior leapt into another's chariot, formed into a mighty phalanx moving forward, away from the castle. Each company had its captain and each battalion had its own commander as the great chariot host pounded behind them. The chariots of its fieldmarshal Summersailor lead the whole beautiful symmetrical display of the handsome warriors, clean and well equipped.

Then the Summersailor raised his Rainbowsword which carved another great rainbow in the sky, as he rode out ahead of the Hawk heroes, marching and riding from the Warwords Castle.

As they rode, the warriors threw their spears up high then caught the spears before they fell down to the earth. Rushspeeding over the plains, in chariotdash they threw their javelins high, the hail of hell. But they caught the javelins before they fell to earth.

Each hero threw his flying daggers high, small sticks of torment if the blades touched flesh. Yet each man caught his dagger without pain and then randomly shot three arrows swiftly from his bow at some of his fellow Hawkwarriors. Each man so targeted, somersaulted, then bent down and stopped the arrows with his shield as easily as children playing leapfrog.

Half of the chariots stood still, the other half turned and drove back towards the Warwords Castle. As fast as hawks at sea after a gull, the charging chariots drew up beside the castle and took on board each chariot, six good soldiers, each one with sword and spear and javelins, armored with mail and helmets. On each cuff were the green and yellow marks of a footsoldier. These strong and stalwart soldiers were speedrushed back to the chariots where the heroes stood. Then the swordsmen threw themselves upon the heroes, anxious to earn the honor of blood scratch.

The heroes with the herolight flashing around them soon made short work of six footmen to one, being careful not to hurt the warriors seriously in disarming them or blood-letting a little.   For these brave foot warriors would one day be backing up the champions on the field of bitter and no-quarter-given combat.

Then the chariots changed places and the ones who carried the foot warriors out to fight the heroes stood still, while the hero fighting champions welcomed, with a great shout, the spear and swordsmen to come aboard. Then drove them back in triumph to face the watching crowds who stood in awe, as the footwarriors cheered their chosen leaders at this great display of skill and coordination.

During this time Summersailor, the viceking and fieldmarshal of the Hawkarmy division, presided over the displays but did not speak.

Winterwarrior, the viceking of the Hillwolves, did not comment during these exercises, but viewed the mock battles with the greatest pleasure, as the Hawkarmy returned to its former camp outside the witches Castle of Warwords.

Among those who rejoined all the watching crowds inside the castle was the Stormleaper, returned from his nocturnal walkings, followed by a dutiful and humble servant carrying a wooden box.

Stormleaper slowly made his way to where the Flyingbat sat at food and wine. Summersailor saw Stormleaper approaching. So, in order to avoid any trouble and to maintain the peace, he moved and came between Stormleaper and Flyingbat.

Then Summersailor whispered to the grim Stormleaper, "Have you still made up your mind to keep your calm?"

"I will not lay a hand nor even touch him," answered the Stormleaper to Summersailor.

The viceking nodded and went his way but watched.

Although the sun had shone for the display, suddenly the long clouds had gathered in the sky as the Stormleaper grimly strode up to the feasting. It seemed like a shadow fell on the assembly just like the black smoke pall that drapes a palace when a king draws near to it on a winter's night.

A silence fell on many who saw Stormleaper and even the dark-robed friends of Flyingbat were frozen and puzzled, quiet and cold-eyed.

The witches paused with slanty eyes of insight, suspicion and fear. Then they drew their cowls around their heads and began to whisper and point as the servant of the Stormleaper shuddered and stumbled. He appeared to splutter and to cough and groan.

Stormleaper, with his servant by his side, solemnly walked to where Flyingbat sat boasting.

Flyingbat stretched and sneered, "Ah, here is the man whose own father was killed by my great brother Oakhill.

"That exhibition of the marching, the charioteering, saber throwing, that martial circus of the slick Hawkarmy was surely a work of battleart designed to scare us, to dismay and frighten us. All that display of sham-fight would have been well named for what it was, just phony show-off.   Ha, ha.

"If Oakhill had been here, he would have challenged each one of those shallow actor-soldiers to single combat after this feast is over and after all have left this hostelry. Oakhill would have defeated them and destroyed them, one by one, and thrown their drained-out bodies into a pit of wolves to eat for breakfast.

"If only my fierce brother had been here, a wolf of wolves, a bear and a furyfighter, unanswerable in times of peace or war, a mighty terror-tyrant and tormentor whom all men fear, yes, even I his brother."

"Then tremble in good faith for he is here," cried the Stormleaper, "Oakhill has arrived, so less of the wordbiting, killtalk and rumorrattling. Less of the sneermongering, for it makes no sense. Oakhill is here. See. He walks beside me. I have brought him here, fresh from the bloodbath combat, to greet his younger brother."

Stormleaper bowed and waved his hand respectfully towards his servant. Flyingbat laughed but others froze in silence, hearing strange sounds and seeing some drops of blood.

Others moved away, shuddering as Flyingbat sneered, "The fool thinks that I do not recognize my brother. I have never even seen this servingman before."

Stormleaper bowed again, "Permit me, Flyingbat."

And suddenly Stormleaper seized the head of Oakhill out of the box, held by his trusty servant, shaking the head by the hair into the face of Flyingbat.

"See, boaster - here is your fierce brother. Recognize him now? Here is the one I have fought in fatal combat."

Men gasped and shuddered in silence as Stormleaper shook out the still-live head of Oakhill, grizzled with pain, snarled up with the grimacing torture of dread death. He threw the head upon the table of Flyingbat.

As the head rolled down onto the table it groaned and spat and splattered blood on the younger brother. The head screamed, "Kill me my brother and save me from this pain."

Then the head opened its mouth and stared and died. And the blood rose up out of the mouth of Flyingbat and he fell dead on the head of his fierce brother.

The witch Landslink rose up and screamed, "You have broken bond."

But Whaleroarer cried out, "No, this was fair. Oakhill was never here. He was killed far from the castle, outside the bond and promise of our agreement. It is just like the murder of my good old dog, Guardhunt."

Windweasel cried, "Dogs, dogs! No! This is war. The time for talking of peace is dead and gone."

And Meteoreyes cried out, "So you want war. Let war be war and choose whom you will serve."

And the Rivershark agreed. Then she stated calmly, "This hostelry is closed. We'll have no more good songs or stories. Make your choices well, for this is your last chance to join the winning host in the great war that lies ahead."

And the servant of Flyingbat quietly handed the Bonespear to the Stormleaper and no one dared to query that the Stormleaper was the winner who had earned the deadly Bonespear.

The Shield of Roar was placed beside Winterwarrior.

Then the War Queen Whitehair laughed, speaking to her three ladies, "As if those hags: those crones of crafty spellsight: the Witches of Kill and mutterers of deceit had ever any intention of speaking peace. What fools men are! Yes, let all men choose well, whether to fight for good or ill. To waiver or to remain loyal to the Truthteller. Whether to support the builders or the destroyers."

Then, in the confusion and the tumult of the warriors leaving the fort, Whitehair, unseen by others, stole away the listening shieldshare with its tassels of forewarning and smuggled it out among the folds and bundles of her outer cloak.

The hardblade Rainbowsword was kept by the Summersailor to help and to support the stealthy killers, his newfound comrades, King Warchariot and the War Queen Snakeknife.

So Summersailor, champion of the Wavewarriors became dedicated to all the treacherous ways of those who deal only in delusion and in deadly mindmadness.

King Warchariot and his War Queen Snakeknife were most pleased to hear this. Those two who held the steadfast plan to rule the world and who baited their mindtraps with strange tricks.

Whitehair looked straight and clearly at Summersailor, who turned aside and spoke to Winterwarrior. Then the warriors of both sides swirled round and turmoiled and the four witches beckoned and called to the warriors with soft entenderments to join the Hillwolves.

But the time for all the wiles of song was over. This was the day of war, for a Yes or No. Yes or No, to help the Make spirits who built up. No or Yes, to support the Break spirits who destroy. And most did make their choice, though a few wavered. Both the Seagulls and the Hillwolves swirled in great disorder.

Then the Summersailor strode out before the Hawks to divide a pathway through the midst of them. He waved his Rainbowsword and the rainbow flew in a straight line down the middle of the army. The Hawkwarriors drew their chariots back, to leave a pathway cleared for the scattering Wavewarriors as they fled. The Seagulls fought a rearguard action against the javelins of the Hillwolf enemy, also protected by Whaleroarer and the Stormleaper with their shields.

***

Some of the Hillwolves were then ushered out in secret through the back entrances of the hostelry, followed by the four witches and their servants.

Meanwhile, the head of Oakhill lay cold and deserted, alone in that great hall. Two heads and a body on the table of fruit and bread and wine where the corpse of the proud and boastful younger brother lay frozen.

The warwinds blew through the empty corridors.

***

Then Whitehair with her three ladies-in-waiting: Streamflower and Maplewine and Willowflame, came to the front entrance of the hostelry and spoke to Summersailor as he stood with Winterwarrior and the Icedragon.

Summersailor bowed his head and addressed his niece Whitehair, "My niece, you and your ladies come with me for we are going over to the army of

Warchariot. Icedragon, our great hero, has also joined us. You will be safe with us and live in honor with Warchariot and his owlwise Queen Snakeknife."

"Why should we live under the protection of those two treacherous and devious murderers? Why have you deserted us and the Wallwave?"

And Summersailor bowed his head and thought. Then he raised his head up high and answered her.

"Wallwave's father had a fatal flaw. A king must always be cautious and cunning. Waterbear had no sense of fear. He had no judgment. Your aunt Springvision and I, his brother, warned and begged and pleaded with the Waterbear not to risk his life at the false funeral.

"Waterbear and Springvision are both dead. I fear the fault of acting without judgment will now fall on the Wallwave and destroy us all.

"Wallwave is young, headstrong and impetuous. His younger brother Stormbolt has not yet finished his training in the arts of war and still learns his war-trade with his greatuncle Shadowhero, so there is little to support Wallwave."

Whitehair replied to her uncle the Summersailor, "You need not fear, for I will tutor him in all the wisdom that a king should know. All he needs now is loyalty and support.

"Is it such a fearful thing for a king to be both brave and reckless of the wiles of witchery? Is it such a fearful thing for a king to be headstrong and impetuous?

"Is it wrong to be loyal, as the Waterbear was to all the Seagull Warriors? I say, let the Wallwave be just like his father. Wallwave has been judged by the oaf Bullaxe to be a man of courage, skill and honor."

As Summersailor thought upon the words of Whitehair, all the Hawkarmy milled round and talked in discontent and in confusion.

***

Now when the Seagulls saw that the Hawkarmy, their crack division, was being given over to fight for their old enemy the Hillwolves, most of the Seagulls fled and drove off in their chariots.

Icedragon stood at the side of the Summersailor as Whitehair spoke, but the inscrutable Icedragon turned his grim face away and did not speak, nor did Whitehair address the Icedragon. Nor did the three ladies speak to anyone.

But frowning, Summersailor shook his head, "The kingdom of the Seagulls has been scattered. See, they have fled to the four corners of the earth. Many have said they are fleeing over the seas. Only my crack division, the Hawkarmy, remain with me and I have been barely able to feed them recently and where is the gold to buy their weapons and accoutrements, unless I accept the offer of Winterwarrior to serve with him under his King Warchariot?"

Then Summersailor added, "Come my niece, Warchariot and his Queen Snakeknife are waiting."

But War Queen Whitehair and her three ladies wore upon them all the accoutrements of warriorwomen and she answered with contempt to the Summersailor, "Then let them wait for death. For treacherous killers will pay the price on their dread judgment day. Your army lies between us and the Wallwave, so stand aside and let us join our king. I am engaged to be married to him. Come. It is not too late to join us. Uncle, please."

Summersailor raised his sword and threw a rainbow road, a highway, through the troops. Then he drove his mighty chariot through the army, with the Icedragon and the Winterwarrior beside him, up to the hill that looked down on the ranks, where he announced to all the gathered Hawks, "Anyone here who does not wish to join me let him step out. I swear I will guarantee him safe journey to rejoin the Wavewarriors in their retreat."

But no one made a move.

Then the Summersailor bowed low to Winterwarrior who welcomed him in joining the many chariots of the Hillwolves.

Whitehair rode through the whole length of the Hawk division with her three ladies: Streamflower, Maplewine and Willowflame, followed only by their small bodyguard. Proudly they rode; looked neither right nor left. They paid no heed to the cheers of the Hawkarmy. Their eyes set straight ahead. Their faces all were grim as they passed Summersailor where he stood with his new leader the owlwise fieldmarshal Winterwarrior. There also stood beside them the grim Icedragon who did not blink an eye.

Yet the vicekings Summersailor and Winterwarrior saluted the War Queen Whitehair as she and her ladies stood up in their chariot and sped away to join Wallwave. But Whitehair gave Winterwarrior and Summersailor only a token glance as she passed by, with a low bow, a sad respect, a longing to remain longer but with a need to go.

For War Queen Whitehair knew that the Summersailor's mind was set for his fate and his eternity. She knew that the witches had woven a trap for Summersailor, of mind manipulations and false sights, so that he could not see what lay ahead, shackles of sorrow, handcuffs of delusion. Summersailor was to be sent down a path that leads to death.

CHAPTER TWELVE
THE KING AND WISDOM

So War Queen Whitehair and her three ladies-in-waiting, with two sun-golden horses before her chariot, drove to the Wallwave's island of deep caves. Great was the pomp and pride of her brave horses. Their tails and manes shook out and shone and tossed as they set out on their familiar path to home, prancing and pounding in joy on the longboat gangway, then sailing across foamy waters to the island where the deep sea caves lay hidden in green weeds. This was the underwater retreat of the Wallwave.

Above them, on that distant snowy island, the former fastness of the Waterbear gleamed in the morning sun. There Wallwave remained in mourning for his dead parents and prayed to the good forces of the universe for true success and wisdom as a king. There the Wallwave hid in misty depths, but sat upon his throne from time to time with garments gleaming in gold and silver sunlight.

Whaleroarer and the Stormleaper had arrived there before Whitehair. They had not been eager to disturb Wallwave with the news that Summersailor and the Hawkarmy had deserted to the enemy.

First, Whitehair moved into her old quarters and slept a heavy sleep of many days. Then later, with her ladies-in-waiting, Willowflame, Streamflower and Maplewine, she went to sit high on the roof of the fastness. There they were joined by the two great heroes and chariotfighters of the Wavewarriors, the Whaleroarer and the Stormleaper.

When Wallwave eventually joined them, Whitehair rushed forward and greeted him with kisses and an embrace. Several other followers who had remained loyal came out before the Wallwave as he sat on his throne, dressed in his splendid robes of gleaming dawn. There they sat eating where they overlooked the sea that churned and chopped in white and seaweed green. There the seabirds, the swooping gulls and crias were crying out.

Whitehair talked with Wallwave and all the Wavewarriors who had stayed loyal to the new king, inheritor of the throne of east and north.

The three ladies-in-waiting bowed low before the young king and dread warrior, for a herolight shone all about the Wallwave. A halo of fire and brightness flashed around him like the haze of the sun hiding behind trees on a summer day.

Whitehair gave the Shieldshare, the Shield of Roar, to the Wallwave as a gift of knowledge and a forewarning of war. Then she sat before the king and told him how Summersailor and the whole Hawkarmy had seen all the wealth of King Warchariot and then deserted to the enemy side.

Wallwave was sad and despondent when he heard this.

It was hard for Whitehair to tell Wallwave of the loss of Summersailor, Wallwave's uncle. She also told of the loss of the Seagull hero, Icedragon with a brain and heart of steel.

But even now she was still not sure of the true fate of Icedragon, whether he had stayed behind as a deserter or as a spy or as a hand of sabotage and redress or revenge. For the Icedragon had not spoken to her afterwards.

So Whitehair told Wallwave of the doubts she had about the Icedragon, "Was he ashamed of his desertion and his treason? Not knowing, I did not dare to speak to him in case the witches or the Winterwarrior had subtly read a clue in his reply, for they have special insights and street magic. We were diverted, waylaid, by the four witches. Most of our armies and some of our champions were even deceived and entrapped by the witches with false visions and by the false hostelry of hospitality. The four witches had transformed themselves into fine ladies and even fooled Stormleaper and the Whaleroarer."

Those two heroes shrugged their shoulders and laughed weakly. They were still puzzled by the feast and answered, "We can only say that the hostesses were lovely. They looked to us like beautiful young ladies. Yet we were not enmeshed like many others who now have lost their way to this far hosting."

Stormleaper told how they had won the Bonespear, the hungry javelin made from the bones of heroes.

"Wallwave, as a tribute to your kingship we give you this Bonespear for your use in battle."

Then Whitehair told how she had seized the shield of warning and, like Stormleaper, she gave the Shield of Roar to the Wallwave for his safety and protection.

"Please take the Shield of Roar to give a fair warning."

"I do not ask for tributes of this kind," said the Wallwave.

"Nevertheless we give wish to give them to you," replied the others.

"Thank you my friends, I will call upon those powers when I need them. You have well avenged your father, Stormleaper, when you took the head of Oakhill in a fair and single combat. I must also avenge my father's murder, even if I die in the long struggle to bind the murderer. I must leave the heirline open for my young brother and leave the islands a safer place for all.

"In this way, honor will be restored to our sad house. But now I need from all of you, a tribute of quite a different kind. I need true wisdom. So now I ask of each of you a saying, a thought of guidance as a gift to me to set me on the right path. As you swear fealty, pay me the tribute of a word of wisdom.

"My enemies will not hear. Only the crias can swoop upon us now and only the waterbeasts can now surround us and creep up on us. Only the whales, seals, crabs and porpoises will hear, as they sun among the fish and fingered seaweeds. If only our enemies were as friendly and harmless. Come, who will be first to pledge his word?"

The Stormleaper bowed, "I pledge my loyalty to you, Wallwave, my word of wisdom is: Set right the wrongs of those who are oppressed. Be just to friend or foe. Take up the cause of the good poor against the wicked rich. Do not let prejudice or passion rule. Be cold and sharp in judgments. In short – be fair."

Likewise, the huge Whaleroarer also pledged his loyalty, "I give you all my help, mighty Wallwave. My word of wisdom is: Do not be rash. Do not take part in drinking feasts. Do not make threats, only fulfill them. Do not set aside good advice because the adviser is poor or old, and do not take advice because the adviser is rich. Think about all ideas, for that is the calmness and dignity of a king. Do not make foes except for a good reason. Do not always try to be first or best. Be calm above the bustle of the rabble or you may become jealous or create envy.

"Do not hold lotteries or any idle competitions. In that way, for every winner there must be created dozens of losers. Only a few winners can take the prize but many will be losers and weep in disappointment. Avoid debt. For this presumes that funds will always be available to pay in future – this will not always be so. Keep clear of dirty tricks of winning and losing.

"Do not be arrogant. Do not be boastful. Do not speak noisily. Above all be cautious."

Then the beautiful warriorwoman Streamflower knelt down before the new young king and bowed.

"I will pray for the Wallwave and for Whitehair. I will pray that you will both be truly happy. I will pray to the universal power of good. I will pray that you may come to understand the things that the powers of good want you to do and pray that you will summon up the courage to do them without the fear of man. Above all, pray."

Then Maplewine knelt down before the king. "Wallwave, I will read to you or sing when you are pondering about deep problems. So read and listen and study to be wise and so you will build reserves of strength and power. Read only the good books, long read of old and deeply revered by all. Life is too short to read the frivolous. Above all, plan."

Then Maplewine bowed low to the Wallwave and the Wallwave smiled and thanked the girl.

And Willowflame also bowed to the Wallwave, her red hair like a burning willow tree.

"This is my tribute of a word of wisdom: Do not take gifts to do the unjust thing. If you do make mistakes take the blame squarely. Do not take what is not yours because of kingship. Restore all things to those who have been robbed.

"Only with good cause grant favors or refuse them. In dealing war, put to death no one because of his poverty and spare the life of no one because of his riches. Do protect from thieves. Above all, be honest."

The Wallwave thanked the girl, bright Willowflame.

Wallwave then turned to his Queen Whitehair, "My future bride, give me your word of wisdom."

Then Whitehair truly advised the Wallwave, the king to be of all the Wavewarriors.

"Do not give out and do not listen to false, idle talks or wicked tittle tattle and rather test the gossip with good questions to find the truth, for truth is all in all. Be kind and loyal to ladies and to friends for we are utterly dependent on you. Do not punish a fool who does not know what he is doing. Do not demand more of any person than he can do with honesty. Do not be a jester or a joker for that is not becoming to a ruler of men. Be serious and thoughtful and be true."

Then the Wallwave said, "I thank all of you for those wisdom words that I will try to follow. Here is my word of wisdom to you all. There are only two forces in the universe, Builders or Breakers: that is Do or Undo: Make or Break. Swords of sun or daggers of night. The eternal powers of good or ill.

"See that you serve only the spirits of good. Every deed that you carry out and every thought that you even think will bounce off the far wall of the universe, where it is multiplied at least ten-fold and comes straight back to hit you in body and spirit so that you will reap ten times what you did sow of good or ill.

"May good works flow to you. And so I say to you, above all, do good."

The End

www.ingramcontent.com/pod-product-compliance
Lightning Source LLC
Chambersburg PA
CBHW060056150626
46556CB00017BA/923